This book should be returned to any branch of the Lancashire County Library on or before the date shown

Lancashire County Library
Bowran Street
Preston PR1 2UX

www.lancash   l/libraries

Lancashire
County Council

SPECIAL MESSAGE TO READERS

THE ULVERSCROFT FOUNDATION
(registered UK charity number 264873)
was established in 1972 to provide funds for
research, diagnosis and treatment of eye diseases.
Examples of major projects funded by
the Ulverscroft Foundation are:-

- The Children's Eye Unit at Moorfields Eye Hospital, London
- The Ulverscroft Children's Eye Unit at Great Ormond Street Hospital for Sick Children
- Funding research into eye diseases and treatment at the Department of Ophthalmology, University of Leicester
- The Ulverscroft Vision Research Group, Institute of Child Health
- Twin operating theatres at the Western Ophthalmic Hospital, London
- The Chair of Ophthalmology at the Royal Australian College of Ophthalmologists

You can help further the work of the Foundation
by making a donation or leaving a legacy.
Every contribution is gratefully received. If you
would like to help support the Foundation or
require further information, please contact:

THE ULVERSCROFT FOUNDATION
The Green, Bradgate Road, Anstey
Leicester LE7 7FU, England
Tel: (0116) 236 4325
website: www.foundation.ulverscroft.com

DREAMS, DEMONS AND DEATH

Psychic investigators are asked to help a man plagued by terrifying dreams that threaten his life . . . A young girl falls into a coma and dreams of another world — and when she wakes, she is no longer human . . . A family of musicians find themselves trapped in a remote village, forced to play the Devil's tune . . . A family celebration ends in a tragic death . . . During a row, a man kills his wife, but finds himself trapped in an even worse relationship . . . Seven stories of dreams, demons and death!

JOHN BURKE

DREAMS, DEMONS AND DEATH

Complete and Unabridged

LINFORD
Leicester

First published in Great Britain

First Linford Edition
published 2014

11878302

A catalogue record for this book is available
from the British Library.

ISBN 978–1–4448–2194–9

Published by
F. A. Thorpe (Publishing)
Anstey, Leicestershire

Set by Words & Graphics Ltd.
Anstey, Leicestershire
Printed and bound in Great Britain by
T. J. International Ltd., Padstow, Cornwall

This book is printed on acid-free paper

Contents

THE BLACKSHORE DREAMER

She stood in the cobbled street leading down to the harbour's edge, and her eyes and inner ears were telling two quite different stories. The view was charming: a group of ladies in blue and pink bonnets provided a splash of colour against the dark-shawled wives of the fishermen, a cart laden with fish boxes lurched unhurriedly up the front of the quay, and beyond the brightly washed cottages a barge with a deep red spritsail swung to starboard around the curve of the harbour wall. Yet at the same time, a silent, suppressed, but mounting hatred jangled within her head.

She went closer to the quayside. As the barge's canvas swished and crumpled down, and the gap between leeboard and wharf narrowed, so the pent-up fury grew. This autumn of 1889 was still mild and mellow, but today its warmth was cut through by freezing anger.

A man began to shout orders from the land to the vessel. She recognised the voice of her brother-in-law and the dominating set of his shoulders.

And within him she recognised another self — twisted by a frenzy as confused as the commands he was bellowing.

'Bring her head round. Hard a-port, you lubbers.'

A protest came from the barge. 'No, master, we're comin' alongside nicely.'

'Do as I say, damn you. Hard to port, and throw me that blasted line.'

The skipper of the barge glared. In his moment of hesitation there was a jarring impact and the groan of tortured woodwork as the stern quarter-board ground against the jetty.

Dr. Caspian came up beside his wife, glanced questioningly at her, and then at the men shouting even wilder orders.

'Sam having trouble?'

Within an instant he was in tune with her, and his next words were silent:

What frightens him so?

Bronwen shook her head, leaning

thankfully on him — on his arm, and on the support of his steady, direct mind.

★ ★ ★

Sam Hillaby turned away to knuckle his eyes as if a spurt of dust or salt spray had momentarily blinded him. When he blinked them open again he was looking straight at a smaller man a few yards away, near one of the mooring bollards. Fury was jolted into life again. The man's face was ordinary enough: middle-aged, slightly wrinkled, with thin lips and irritable yet humorous blue eyes framed in a shock of sandy hair. But when Bronwen and Dr Alex Caspian aligned themselves carefully with Sam Hillaby's viewpoint they witnessed that ordinary face becoming oddly dreamlike — shifting, disturbed and blurred, as though overlaid with other remembered features or possessed in broad daylight by a mocking, encroaching ghost.

The features sharpened again to normality as the two of them withdrew from Sam's mind and used their own eyes. Now it was the other's turn to show anger. His gaze was following a lean, bearded man in a long frock coat who had come striding down the street, approaching the barge as two of its crew leapt ashore and prepared to make fast and begin unloading.

'A safe journey?' The voice was deep and persuasive, like that of a well-rehearsed revivalist preacher.

'Aye, sir.'

'Brought us luck again, sir.'

'I rejoice to hear it.'

They each pressed his hand; and it might have been coins or some other offering that were slipped through in this fashion. Bronwen half expected her brother-in-law to turn on his men and berate them for not getting on with their work. But Sam also sought the man's smile, before directing another vindictive glance at the smaller figure by the bollard. It was all unspoken, but mentally audible to Bronwen and Caspian.

They turned away, worried by their own mental intrusion, but even more worried by the extremity of Sam's distress. His wife had not been mistaken in summoning them to Blackshore.

In the years since their first exhausting experiences of thought transference and psychic intuition they had learned to restrict use of their shared talent to cases of dire need. What was coming to be warily acknowledged in scientific circles as telepathy was a rare faculty, and one not to be squandered. Capable in moments of crisis of a powerful mutual resonance, they could probe into afflicted minds and distinguish between psychological stress and supernatural dangers. Sometimes those dangers had threatened to engulf their own being: they had narrowly escaped the tug of many an occult whirlpool beyond the fringe of normal human consciousness, had faced and been almost overcome by human torment and supernatural menace, and justified the expenditure of their own psychic powers only by saving a soul here, someone's sanity there. But it was a stern principle that they should not make too free of other people's minds and emotions, should not casually eavesdrop

— should enter only by invitation.

When Bronwen's sister Angharad called them in, it was without understanding how they worked together or how delicately, in a harmony of thought, they could insinuate themselves into the consciousness and unconsciousness of others to disentangle their obsessions, as a surgeon might disentangle warped fibre tissue or a threatening strangulation. But she had always known that Bronwen was gifted with strange mental powers, and that since marriage to Alex Caspian she had somehow achieved a great expansion of those powers. She needed their help; and needed it to be unobtrusive.

'Sam won't say a sensible thing about it to anyone,' she had confided last night, after their arrival. 'Won't even speak to the doctor — seems to have taken right against this. But there's something wrong . . . inside . . . inside his *head*.'

They wanted to help her, but Sam would certainly not knowingly let them in. And they did not like catching people off-guard, as they had briefly done this morning.

8

When they were well out of earshot of those clustering about the harbour, Bronwen said: 'There's a specific target for that hatred of his.'

'The taut little chap with the sandy hair and the twinkle?'

'I'm glad you noticed the twinkle.'

'Could be a devilish one. Pleasure in other people's discomfiture.'

'Is that how it struck you?'

'Frankly, no.' Caspian tugged at the sharp hatchet end of his trimmed beard. 'He seemed somewhat prickly — sure of himself and impatient with those who don't match up to his standards, I'd guess — but not a man deliberately out to cause distress. Perhaps he's only a focus for whatever it is that's troubling Sam.'

'And how do we find out what it is?'

'Your sister did say something about him somehow being haunted, but it was only because she couldn't think of any other way of putting it.'

They sauntered back towards the house down its sheltered lane. A man might well imagine himself haunted by many a phantasm in huddled little Blackshore.

There could, also, be echoes beyond human imagining. So many creatures had been spawned on or clung to this stormy eastern shore of England; and it took strange men to cling here rather than seek greater comfort inland — men whose stubborn will to survive might outlive their own deaths. Early settlers had knapped flint into harpoon heads for fishing in the creeks, and then done battle with more savage waters. Warrior tribes had followed across those same North Sea waters to harass them and settle in their turn. Here strange freaks from the sea lived on in legend; wan moons presaged disaster; phosphorescent bones drifting in on many a tide told of drowned husbands and sons, fishermen and fighting men. Who could deny that ancient wraiths lived on behind the rows of cottages, or skimmed the surfaces of inlets trailing secretively across the marshes? Shadows had, over the centuries, accumulated more substance than ephemeral flesh and blood.

Caspian said: 'Perhaps we should ask Sam outright.'

'You'll not get much response from folk along this coast by asking questions outright. If Sam hasn't confided fully in Angharad — '

' — he won't confide in us,' he finished for her.

'So we have to lure him out with a special bait.'

'Or trespass,' said Caspian softly. They reached the house and he set his hand on the latch of the side door. 'Go in deep,' he said, 'and capture the parasite which feeds on him in the darkness.'

Angharad looked up hopefully as they came in. She had been able to tell them so little, yet obviously she had been praying that after their stroll through Blackshore this morning they would somehow come up with an explanation and a miraculous antidote.

Bronwen wasted no time in comforting generalisation. 'You told us that Sam was being haunted in some way. You didn't tell us about this hatred that's got ahold of him.'

'Hatred?' Her sister tried to stare her out, then lowered her gaze. Their faces were so alike in so many ways, and they both had glowing auburn hair and the same fey, green Welsh eyes. But whereas Bronwen was steely and direct, Angharad had always been the shy, worrying member of the family. 'I . . . I've tried to pretend that it wasn't that bad. That he didn't hate me, couldn't *really* hate me.'

'I wasn't talking about you, my dear. It's some man down at the harbour he's angry with.'

'As well as with me, then.'

Caspian's arm slid round Bronwen's shoulders. Although their thoughts did not deliberately mingle, the embrace gave his tone a new intensity. 'Angharad, this is the first time you've mentioned anything about Sam hating you.'

'But there I was telling you, just this morning, before you went out.' The plaintive Welsh lilt, never quite lost in spite of Angharad's exile on this far side of the country, rose and fell. 'He has these dreams, see, and when he wakes up he wants to get them out of his system — only he won't let himself, won't talk to me. Just goes on how there's things that ought

12

never to be here, and somehow makes me feel it's me who puts them here.'

'No,' said Bronwen quietly. 'You didn't mention that.'

'With thinking about it all the time, maybe there's forgetting I was to speak out properly. He can't abide the house, see, but he won't go away. I wish he *would* go away.'

Bronwen was shocked. 'You want him to leave you?'

'No,' wailed Angharad. 'Just for him to be the way he was. Going off on one of his barges up the coast, and enjoying it and enjoying coming home to me. Instead of letting his men carry the cargoes, and his staying at home hating every minute, and getting everything wrong, and saying he . . . I . . . '

They waited, until Caspian had to prompt her gently: 'Saying what?'

'That he daren't leave me on my own.'

Before they could pursue the matter further there came three sharp raps on the front door knocker. Angharad went to answer, and returned to the sitting room with a man behind her.

He was the one they had seen Sam close to on the waterfront; the one whose shifting features had drawn Sam's rage.

'Dr Petersen,' Angharad was saying, 'this is my sister, Mrs Caspian. And Dr Caspian.'

The tight little mouth twitched a brusque conventional smile. '*Doctor . . . ?*'

'Of philosophy,' said Caspian.

'Hmm. Need some of that myself, in these parts. Now, Mrs Hillaby, if I could just have a few minutes of your time.'

She led him away, across the passage to the small, little-used parlour. 'Won't be long.' She tried to sound cheerful as she called back to Bronwen and Caspian.

Silently they consulted each other; found the bewilderment just as taxing as the telepathic strain, and sat back without another word, waiting for Angharad to rejoin them.

When she came in she was transformed. 'Bron . . . Alex . . . I'm going to have a baby.'

Bronwen threw her arms around her sister.

'That's wonderful. Wonderful. Sam will be so pleased.'

Angharad stiffened against her. 'I hope so. Oh, there's hoping I am.'

'But isn't that what he's always wanted — a boy, to follow him in the business and keep the Hillaby name afloat?'

'It'll be a girl.'

In the doorway, Dr Petersen snorted. 'These women, they never look on the bright side.' He fastened the catch of his battered leather bag. 'For all we know at this stage, Mrs. Hillaby, you may present your husband with two boys to carry on the trade.'

Bronwen laughed. 'Come now, doctor, you'll really alarm her.'

'No need for alarm. Fine, healthy young woman. Provided,' — his thin lips tightened almost to invisibility — 'she follows my advice and not that of the old wives of Blackshore. Or our resident charlatan.'

Angharad edged away towards the window.

'Old wives,' said Caspian, 'with their potions? Yes, I imagine you get a fair share around here.'

15

'Indeed we do. Place still reeks with old sailors' superstitions, and others their womanfolk have brewed up for them. Sometimes I have the feeling this village stopped in the Middle Ages and doesn't care for visitors from the late nineteenth century. Do you know, to this day when a man's at sea his wife at home will never throw away an eggshell without smashing it into tiny pieces.'

'Because half an eggshell's enough of a craft for a witch to sail out in and destroy his boat.'

'Dr Caspian, I gather you're well versed in such idiocies. But here things are even worse. On top of all the other problems we've got a damned quack, a damned clever one, posturing through the streets and profiting from their credulity. Undoing all the work I try to do and making a shameful living out of it. You know these same gullible creatures used to throw a handful of coins overboard at the start of each fishing voyage — '

'To buy a good catch.'

'Quite so. But now we have this impostor collecting the money himself, laying his hands on their heads, telling the poor fools that *he* will guarantee the catch for them. Playing God Almighty. Good catch and safe return.'

'And relieving afflictions which have plagued some sufferers for years.' Angharad turned back towards them. 'You know it, Dr Petersen. You know that Healer Monckton has brought genuine relief to many.'

'*Healer* Monckton. Only relief he brings is after I've done the hard work. And hard work it is, I assure you. Persuading them to follow a proper medical regimen, when the moment my back's turned he's there wheedling a tribute out of them and promising they'll all get up and walk and never have another ache or pain in their lives. I swear to you, I'll drive that mountebank out of Blackshore if it's the last thing I do.'

'This Monckton,' Caspian ventured, 'if he can persuade people to heal themselves, surely that's as valid a cure as the orthodox medical one?'

'*If* . . . You're a doctor of philosophy, sir. I'm a doctor of medicine. I make my mistakes like any man in any profession — but I think folk stand a better chance in my care than they do with a course of charms, amulets and incantations.' He swung his case against his thigh as he turned for the passage. 'I'll be in again the day after tomorrow, Mrs Hillaby. And I hope *you* won't dabble with faith healers and mesmerists and old witches with their fish kettles.'

The front door slammed behind him.

From the window they saw him pause on the edge of the pavement. Sam Hillaby was approaching his own front door. The two men bristled at each other like two dogs about to snarl their way into a fight. Then, again like two dogs, they circled around each other and went their ways.

Again the door slammed. Sam came in and said: 'What's that butcher been doing here?'

'Sam, I've wonderful news.' Angharad was half ecstatic, half apprehensive. 'Wonderful news.'

Caspian took Bronwen's arm and began tactfully to lead her out of the room so that the two could be alone

18

together. But before they had closed the sitting room door behind them, Angharad was rushing on: 'Sam, love, I'm going to have a baby.'

There was the briefest of silences. And then Sam said: 'Are you, now? And who's the father?'

* * *

Supper that evening was a sombre affair during which Sam and his wife exchanged hardly a word. All Caspian's careful attempts at conversation fell into an unresponsive void. The oil lamp swung from its bracket in the beam above the table, casting new swatches of darkness down Sam's weather-beaten face, and emphasising the pouches under Angharad's tearful eyes.

When the gloomy meal was over, Sam went out into the street and leant against the jamb of the front door, smoking his pipe. Caspian contemplated joining him, then saw, at an angle from the window, a tall figure pacing the far side of the lane. It was the bearded man identified by

Angharad as Healer Monckton. In the autumn twilight he made a dignified figure moving sombrely past lamp-lit windows until, with sudden purpose, he changed direction to cross the lane and come to a halt before Sam.

Caspian longed to summon Bronwen quickly to his side so that they could concentrate their attention on Sam and fathom what was passing between him and this character, so much detested by the village doctor. But there was no time. Bronwen was in the kitchen helping Angharad with the dishes and trying to help her in her misery at her husband's reaction to what ought have been joyful news.

Only a few remarks passed between Sam and Monckton. Then Monckton put his right hand on Sam's left shoulder and looked earnestly into Sam's face. He might have been implanting a comradely message of reassurance. When he had paced on, Sam remained smoking more placidly, his shoulder propped more comfortably against the woodwork.

Now Caspian ventured out.

The evening air was cool but pleasant, stirred only by a salt-tinged breeze off the sea, carrying with it a tang of herring from the harbour smokehouses. Clouds above the cottage chimneys were brightened by a shrouded, climbing moon. It was as tranquil an evening picture as the one Bronwen had contemplated this morning.

Caspian said bluntly: 'We couldn't help overhearing what you said to Angharad. Sam . . . what's the matter?'

Sam puffed on his pipe until the pungent smell of course shag overrode that of smoked fish and salty breeze.

'Who says anything's the matter?'

'You can't have forgotten what you said.'

'Maybe I could.' The pipe added a wreath of smoke to streamers curling from the chimney. 'Or maybe I could just have been saying what was in my mind, and . . . ' He choked. Perhaps he had inhaled too deeply. Or perhaps not. 'I fancy I heard myself saying . . . but I don't see what it's got to do with . . . I mean . . . '

Caspian was remorseless. 'You were given news to warm the heart. A son or daughter as consummation of your love for Angharad. What you've always wanted: someone to carry on after you.'

'Carry on?' Sam echoed tonelessly. 'There's been a sight too much of that, if you ask me — carrying on.'

'Sam, what's got into you?'

'Damned if I know.' Sam's slow local mumble was abruptly alive and trembling. 'I don't know what *she's* up to, or what *I'm* up to or anything. Don't know why I should be beset by these notions. But there's something, that I can tell you, something in *there*.' He jabbed despairingly with the bowl of his pipe towards the door of his home, so that a little shower of sparks sprayed out and glimmered to the ground. 'In there, in that pest-ridden house.'

'But Bronwen's often told me how fond you always were of your house, you and Angharad.'

'Me. And Angharad.' Sam forced the words out with an air of disbelief. Then he groaned: 'Something's wrong in there, something I can't be bearing. But something I don't dare leave. It gets at me . . . but when I'm away, how do I know it's not getting at Angharad? Getting at her, leading her into bad ways?'

'She's never said anything to Bronwen about that.'

'No? Well she wouldn't, would she? Or if she did, all that woman-to-woman chatter, you think your Bronwen would tell *you?*'

'Yes,' said Caspian.

Sam snorted and pushed himself away from the wall. He tapped out the dottle from his pipe, pushed the door open, and then hesitated on his own threshold. 'I don't suppose you believe in haunted houses, would you?'

It was a question to which Caspian, of all men, was least likely to give a reassuring, tidy answer. Did he believe in haunted houses? Of course. But haunted by what — and how much of his belief and experience could be simplified for Sam's benefit? There had been that house in Herefordshire where a resonance of ancient good had been misguidedly

23

exorcised to admit a force of bestial evil; but had that truly been a haunting, or a spiritual miasma infecting only those prone to such diseases? His first meeting with the woman who was now his wife had been in a village possessed — but not by what Sam or most men like his would call ghosts.

Tentatively he said: 'I believe some people foster terrors in their own minds. And others are sensitive to the vibrations of old terrors left on the air.'

'Left on the air?' Sam stayed quite still for a moment. 'It can happen, then? Just like a bit of an old tune that gets stuck in your head, and you can't get rid of it?'

'The question is: what led you to hear it in the first place, and then feel compelled to retain it?'

Sam grunted incomprehension, and went on indoors.

In bed that night, in darkness tinged only by a faint line of moonlight down the side of the little dormer window, and in silence only broken by the lulling rustle of the tide against the harbour wall, Caspian and Bronwen lay side by side, wide awake, their hands linked.

After a long silence Caspian said: 'There's nothing loose in the house.'

'Not yet, anyway.'

No tremor, no resonance. But so often there was no echo of a tragic or violent past until the right instrument was there to catch it — an aeolian harp picking up the undying whisper of fear of sadness.

'If there's an answer,' said Caspian, 'it may emerge from Sam's dreams.'

They could remotely feel the threshing and stumbling of Sam's thoughts and half-thoughts, characteristic of that dizzying interlude between waking and sleeping; a jumble of meaningless words and phrases, a sudden slip and the catch of breath as one seems to slide from a doorstep, a quickening of the heart and then a slowing again.

Bronwen murmured: 'Ought we to intrude? Have we the right?'

'Angharad wants us to do all we can, that's why she sent for us.'

'Yes, but Sam himself . . . '

'They are one. Just as staunchly as you and I are one. You know that. They're one and they wish to remain one. So if Angharad has asked, then she has asked for both of them. We must do it.'

There was no further speech between them. They waited, poised, until the rhythm of Sam's mind in the bedroom at the front of the house took on its regular pulse of sleep.

And then the changing rhythm of dreams.

Caspian and Bronwen probed their way unobtrusively into a mind now beginning to conjure up fleeting scenes and shadow. Their perceptions sharpened as they adjusted to the tempo of Sam's nightmare. The tuning fork of his mind began to sing, high-pitched and insistent.

The house was still here about them. Yet at the same time its walls were transparent; there was nothing to stop them drifting out into the night. And nothing to stop things coming in from the darkness, from the sea. Sam's mind flinched, twisted, then was tussling with the old horror far out of this period of time: a horror racing in from the restless waters, old and gone before ever one stone of this early Victorian house was laid, yet now co-existent with it, threatening it and its inhabitants.

A distant horn sounded a fearsome chord, like some sea monster breaking surface and trumpeting its wrath. Faint screams drifted across the harbour entrance, as raucous as the screeching of gulls, carried away on a flurry of wind.

Sam was still in the house, aware of his surroundings, his bed and his wife beside him. Yet somehow he was beyond the no longer solid wall, and his wife was cowering behind him as he strode down to the shore. Out of the night came the bray of the horns again, and now rose a vision of a dragon's head and square sail, and of helmeted barbarians waiting to jump into the shallows and storm up the shingle.

Now the dream contracted. Everything was crushed into one place at once. Sam was grappling with a bearded warrior on the shore — not some tall Viking, but a short, savage little Jutish figure jabbing out with the dreaded short axe of his tribe. Sam fought to get a grip on the haft. That iron fang would be lethal if it had a chance to bite: slicing him down the breastbone so that the invader could tear his ribs back and then splay them out on the ground in the bloody semblance of the spreadeagle.

Then it would be Angharad's turn.

But for her it would not be the axe. She would be pierced by flesh and muscle, not iron. Already, as he fought, Sam knew that the enemy was grinning lustfully past him, marking the woman out as his prey.

They staggered, fell, struggled up again.

Now Sam was facing in the opposite direction, so that he could see his wife only a few feet away. His wife, Angharad, naked and unprotected; but not cowering now, not terror-stricken. She was answering the despoiler's grin, half crouching, her legs obscenely crooked, inviting him to despatch her husband quickly and come to ravish her, tear and foul her, bellow a great rutting bellow she could share . . .

The man's sweating face was close to Sam's. It would all be ended in a few seconds. He knew the face. Beneath the tangle of beard he surely knew the leering features, the mockery and the mean-mouthed greed.

A great shudder ran through Sam's body and mind. And he woke up.

Through the bleariness of his opening eyes Caspian and Bronwen glimpsed Angharad's face turning towards him on the pillow. She reached out a comforting, loving hand. They felt the shock of Sam's desire for her, and then his revulsion as faint reflections of his dream brightened again into a swirling fantasy of her naked body, luring him on and then mockingly rejecting him.

Caspian drew back, carrying Bronwen with him. They had trespassed long enough. It was unthinkable that they should linger into the couple's waking love and jealousy.

But they themselves lay awake for a long time, silently communing until they were too weary and had to resort to drowsy whispers.

'The Danes invaded this coast so many times.'

'And settled here in the end. Look at some of the village names.'

'And the hair and faces of some of the villagers.'

'Terror like that can resound in the air forever.'

'And yet . . . '

Bronwen was unconvinced.

Caspian voiced her uncertainties. 'It wasn't so much Sam responding to an ancient echo as Sam himself *summoning it up.*'

'Against his will.'

'Then on whose command?'

★　★　★

When they came downstairs in the morning, Sam had already left the house to supervise his barge's loading for the turn-around. They found it hard to meet Angharad's wan eyes, knowing so much as they did now about Sam, but not nearly enough. She was too diffident to ask when they hoped to work the miracle she was waiting for.

Sam returned as they were finishing

breakfast. With no more than a gruff pretence of a 'Good morning' he announced aggressively: 'I'll be skippering the *Centaur* myself this trip. A Sunderland run. So I'd best be getting my tackle together.'

'You can't just go making your mind up just like that,' protested Angharad as he made for the stairs. 'No sense in it, not like that, just on the spur of the moment.'

'You've nagged me often enough lately to put to sea again.'

'Yes, but — '

'Do me good, you said. So it might, a week away from this cursed place. I'll try it, anyway.'

'But love, we've got Bronwen and Alex staying.'

'Another good reason for me to get away. They can keep an eye on you, see you don't get into mischief.'

It might have been a joke; but it wasn't.

He thumped up the stairs.

Angharad strangled a sob. 'What am I going to do?'

When Sam reappeared with his ditty bag and a roll of bedding under one arm, Caspian signalled to Bronwen that she should stay with Angharad. Over the washing-up and the household chores she might get some unexpected lead on Sam's strange turn of temperament. At the same time he would walk down to the boat with Sam.

For a moment it looked as if Sam might object to Caspian's company. But there was no real ground for protest. Caspian offered to carry the roll of blankets and fell easily into Sam's stride. They went down the lane and then down the street in silence until Caspian asked, as casually as possible: 'Have you any idea what was on the site before your house was built?'

Sam glanced sideways at him. 'What makes you ask?'

'I was curious. It's set a bit apart from the rest of the village. I wonder if it belonged to anyone special. Or if anything ever happened there.'

'Happened?' Sam was determined to give nothing away.

'Things left on the air,' Caspian used the phrase again and waited for a reaction.

'You feel it then? In our house?' Sam wanted an answer yet, Caspian sensed, did not want one.

'I merely wondered.'

And was still wondering. A village of this age just had to have its community of ghosts. Even in daylight he could feel their presence in this street. Widows of long ago, keening for their men lost in a gale. A sad child, breathing her last in a hovel at the end of an alley, terrified by the sound of the plague cart rattling closer over the cobbles. The place was alive with the dead. But in Sam's clean, shipshape house he had detected no murmur of anything — no persistent phantom or any other alien presence.

Sam made an effort. 'Alex, I'm sorry if I've not been a very good host. But I do *need* to get away. After last night . . . ' He stopped, then went on hurriedly: 'I got to thinking. Angharad's right: I've got stale, I need to get away, I'll feel easier if you're there, and it's only for *me* that the house is . . . spoiling things. And maybe it'll be right by the time I get back.'

They had reached the quay. A mass of

coprolite from the crag pits two miles down the coast was being loaded. Sam watched the process for a few minutes, and imperceptibly relaxed. This was the setting he most loved; this, his natural rhythm.

'We'll be a sight dirtier on the way back,' he confided. 'We'll be loaded with coal for the gasworks up-river.'

It was all so solid and four-square and matter-of-fact. On a day like this Caspian found it hard to think of his brawny companion being tormented by jealous nightmares in the dark small hours.

'Who have you put in command this voyage, Captain Hillaby?'

Monckton, tall and imperious, had joined them on silent feet. There was something patronising in his attentive smile.

Sam said: 'I'm running her myself this time.'

Monckton looked startled. Caspian felt the tremor of disapproval — yet why should this man approve or disapprove of the harbour's routine and those who worked it?

'I thought you had been delegating such duties recently and concentrating on supervision here in Blackshore.'

'Aye. But it's time that I felt the deck under my feet again.'

Caspian thrust out his hand to seize Monckton's attention. 'I don't think we've met. Alexander Caspian.'

'My wife's brother-in-law,' Sam added.

Monckton's hand was cool and firm. The intensity of the contact told Caspian at once that here was someone to be reckoned with. However Dr Petersen might snarl his dislike, this man had undoubted powers. As a faith healer he would assuredly persuade people to fall into the ways he prescribed. Might even have occult powers. During his career of investigating psychic phenomena, and at the same time relentlessly exposing fake mediums, spiritualists and ill-equipped dabblers in shoddy necromancy, Caspian had learned to identify the aura given off by other gifted or accursed psychic practitioners: a force for healing or for malevolence.

The man was blandly appraising him.

Those liquid eyes were almost too winning. His smile hinted that he suspected Caspian's challenge and felt confident of coping with it. Such a man could be of benefit to an inbred, isolated community of this kind; or an incubus draining it of vitality.

Caspian said: 'You appear to be alarmed by Sam's decision to sail away from Blackshore for a while.'

'My dear sir, why should I be alarmed? It came as a surprise, that's all.'

'And the local sailormen aren't supposed to spring surprises on you?'

Monckton's smile grew less amiable. 'I have no jurisdiction over their comings and goings. As a friend I help them when it's in my humble power, but it's not for me to dictate what's good for them, or bad for them.'

'If you were to press Sam, in his own interest, do you think he'd accept your advice and stay?'

'Why should I want to *press* him?'

Demonstrating his indifference, Monckton waved idly at Sam, who was moving away from the loading hoist. Let him go or stay, as he chooses, said the graceful turn of the wrist.

Bronwen and Angharad were on their way down the street to watch the preparations. They kept their distance, as if Angharad did not wish to risk distracting Sam or provoking any unpredictable outburst. For his part, Caspian was only too glad to be distracted. He contemplated the delightful picture: two sisters, so different yet so complementary, so attractive, with Bronwen's bronze hair more deeply burnished than Angharad's, yet their mutual balance achieved so perfectly by Angharad's palely glowing skin.

Hair, skin and eyes suddenly burned brighter. There was a flash of unleashed sexual appetite: a dazzling vision, taking Caspian's breath away, of bare limbs writhing, a spreadeagle of Angharad howling and quivering with desire.

Then there were just two young married women strolling demurely down the slope, heads turned towards each other, pretending unawareness of the appreciative male scrutiny.

Sam had seen them; paused, and hunched away.

Monckton went on studying them with his imperturbable earnestness. Then he too was deflected, concentrating all at once on quite a different girl. Squatting barefoot on the doorstep of a wooden hut, she was busily stitching a torn net until he called to her. 'Ah, there, Miss Emily.' His arms spread wide as if to draw her into his embrace. She simpered, swept the net from her knees, picked her way pertly round a little heap of cork floats, and trod lightly over the cobbles in an arc between Sam and the quayside.

There was a howl of execration from one of the men waiting with a water cask at his side. 'You cussed bitch! Look what she's gone an' done!'

Sam stared, and went pale.

Caspian said: 'What's wrong? Whatever — '

'Oh dear.' Monckton bowed his leonine hand. 'How stupid of me. My fault entirely. How could I have been so thoughtless . . . '

38

'You seen that?' The seaman stood rigid on the spot.

'Right between us and the boat,' groaned Sam. 'With nothing to her feet.'

Bronwen and Angharad reached Caspian. In an undertone Angharad explained: 'No East Coast mariner will go to sea if a bare-footed woman crosses the path between him and his boat.'

'Tomorrow, damn it,' Sam was lamenting. 'It'll have to be tomorrow now. Twenty-four hours late we'll be.' He turned in supplication towards Monckton, who was spreading his hands in unctuous apology. 'You couldn't . . . well, lift it? Do something to cancel it out?'

Monckton flickered a smile at Caspian. 'They really do take me for some kind of magician. It's most embarrassing.'

He went to Sam, bowing further apologies. Then his hand touched Sam's shoulder in a consolatory gesture. His fingers tightened as he gazed commandingly into Sam's eyes. From a distance the stance was friendly enough, but with cold clarity Caspian saw the pose of the mesmerist, establishing rapport and ready to begin incantatory phrases.

Bronwen was with him, but not swiftly enough. They caught only a few snatches of soothing invocation.

'If fate so wills it . . . only a day . . . you were not truly ready today . . . '

Mutely Bronwen and Caspian plucked at echoes.

Press him. Why should a fragment of one of Caspian's own remarks linger, rebounding and resounding like that? And then the rest: *not truly ready . . .*

They asked each other in unison: *not ready for what?*

★ ★ ★

That evening Caspian again forced his company on Sam. In grumpy mood, Sam had declared that he would go out for an hour or so to the Anchor Inn. Whether or not he was deceived by Caspian's casual agreement that he, too, could do with a couple of pints of ale, he could hardly repulse him.

The bar of the tavern was crammed and smoky. Sam added to the fug by lighting up his pipe and champing on the stem. He sank the contents of a pint tankard in one gulp and pounded on the counter for another. Clearly he was in a mood to drink himself into a stupor.

Caspian tried to drink along with him and joke with him, but Sam was in no state for jokes.

'If I don't soon get away from here,' he growled at one stage, 'I'll not be responsible for . . . ' And then, moist-eyed over his fifth refill, 'Not safe to go, not with these scum, not with that . . . *that* one . . . ' He was angry and maudlin at the same time.

The door opened and the local coastguard came in, off duty and thirsty. He waved to a mate in the corner and slapped Sam on the back. Sam's head came round slowly and jerkily. Through his tipsy confusion he twitched and reacted; then groped for meaning. Caspian made the effort to see through Sam's eyes. All he glimpsed was a face he half recognised — certainly not that of the coastguard — and a flash of something incongruously like a sabre, rising and dazzling Sam.

'You grubby bastard. You goat, you lousy lickerish bloody goat.'

Sam was aiming a blow at the coastguard, who dodged and caught his arm good-humouredly. 'Off with you, now, Sam. You'd best be staggering home.'

Sam struggled, but Caspian took his other arm and steered him towards the door.

'Mind the fresh air don't bring him down,' the landlord called after them.

* * *

They reeled home. Angharad took Sam's weight, grumbling affectionately, and led him upstairs, with Caspian pushing from behind. When she came down again she was half smiling.

'Sorry to bring him home in such a state,' said Caspian.

'I'd sooner he was this way than . . . ' She would not finish.

When Bronwen and Caspian had gone

to bed they stretched themselves out and stared at the ceiling, pallid in the filtered light from outside.

'Will he be too drunk to have any dreams, do you think?'

'He may have some particularly lurid ones.'

Her hand sought his. Her mind rubbed lovingly against his. Then they let the infinitely sensitive antennae of their consciousness probe out, catching a tremor of Angharad's mind then a blurred memory of the tavern from Sam's. At the moment he was not quite sure of where he was.

Caspian murmured: 'There's still not a hint of any atavistic recession or recurrence in the building itself. It contains no latent occult memory. Whatever currents run, it's Sam who sets them in motion.'

And he added the thought: *when prompted to do so.*

They felt the drunken reelings of Sam's head. Then through the groundswell of nausea a picture began to emerge, like an uncanny still refection on the surface of a storm-flecked sea.

A young man with a tricorne hat, trim white trousers and a blue jacket was leading a small party of men up the street. They were swinging heavy cudgels, prepared for trouble. Their lieutenant carried a cutlass, which he raised as he approached Sam, so that it flashed and stung Sam's eyes. But the village was in darkness, so how could it flash; how did Sam come to be out in the street?

As if to explain it to himself, he heard a tumult of voices within his own head. His neighbours were crying, their wives screaming.

'It's the press gang! Bolt your doors!'

The little naval detachment made no attempt to break down doors to either side, but came to a halt in front of Sam.

'Take him,' snapped the officer.

Take him . . . to the waiting ship, to misery on the high seas, flogging, disease, probably death. Never to see home again for at least five years.

Sam made a grab for the cutlass. The lieutenant swung it out of reach, then struck him across the shoulder. Sam lashed out. The ratings of the press gang hurled themselves on him and bore him down. Before they could drag him away he saw Angharad drawing close to the lieutenant, smiling grotesquely, lifting her lips to his. She was ready without more ado to wave farewell to one man and a delirious welcome to another.

This time the leader had no beard. This time the face was unmistakeable. Though younger and more arrogant, the features were unquestionably those of Dr Petersen.

Sam woke and reeled from his bed to vomit into the washstand bowl.

★ ★ ★

In the pale dawn Caspian said: 'Our puppet master must have calculated that Sam needed one more prod to drive him over the edge. Now he'll be hoping that Sam's ready.'

Healer Monckton. Silently Caspian denounced the man with the savagery he reserved for insidious dealers in the black arts — not white magicians and healers, but infectors. Monckton, self-seeking and self-glorifying witch doctor and mesmerist, who had contrived a delay in Sam's embarkation to allow time for one more conjuration of jealousy and hatred.

'And who on the spur of the moment,' mused Caspian, 'picked up a phrase of mine and refashioned it for implanting in Sam's mind. *Press him*! Let him be tormented by the notion of the press gang — another parting, another betrayal.'

They must sweep clean this building, which sheltered no intrinsic wickedness, but the deliberately poisoned recesses of Sam's mind. And they both sensed, from Monckton's hurried snatching at the chance concept, that there might not be much time left.

★ ★ ★

Sam was pasty-faced as he set off down to the harbour to catch the tide, showing no signs of looking forward to the voyage. Little was said as they went to see him off — his wife, Bronwen and Caspian.

Freight and his own immediate necessities had been stowed aboard. All was well. Calm sea and prosperous voyage: what else was there to wish him, aloud or in prayer?

For a mile offshore the sea was steely bright, then blended into a sullen band of grey, which spilt over the horizon into unclouded but unshining sky. A couple of fishermen studied sky and water, nodding unspoken mysteries to each other. A few locals sat in their doorways. The girl who had trodden barefoot across Sam's path the previous morning looked down at her grimy toenails, blushed, and scurried indoors.

★ ★ ★

Monckton had positioned himself by the for'ard mooring bollard like a prophet ready to pounce at a benediction.

Sam broke awkwardly away from his companions and veered close to Monckton. The three of them did not hear what he said, but Caspian caught Monckton's reply.

'I'm sure all will be well now.'

The intensity of Bronwen's and Caspian's concentration must have jarred a corner of his awareness. He shot them a quick glance. Instinctively they scrambled their thoughts into incoherence until, moving discreetly away from Angharad, Caspian could say in undertone: 'He has lit another fuse into Sam's mind. This one is timed to blast Sam out forever, so that Monckton can take possession.'

'Possession of what?'

Caspian nodded almost imperceptibly at Angharad.

Now he knew. It had been Monckton's lust that he sensed when Bronwen and Angharad walked down this very street only yesterday. At the time it had seemed like a drifting shred of Sam's dreams. But the priapic fever had been Monckton's — a burning desire for Angharad, which would scorch anyone who got in his way.

Bronwen was silently communicating: *But she'd never let him near, she wouldn't dream of it.*

Dream is just what she'll do, when he's ready. He's an adept at inculcating

dreams. Angharad is what he wants, and when Sam has been disposed of and when he's ready and has made her ready . . .

Sam and Monckton stood side by side looking up into the barge's rigging. Monckton's hand once more sought Sam's shoulder.

'None of Sam's phantoms really came from the past,' said Caspian decisively. 'All those nightmares have been *priming him for what's yet to come.*'

Very soon now. They knew it; and moved closer behind the two men on the quayside.

Sam sprang aboard. The barge boy was stopping over the stern rope, shaking a coil loose as the other was freed from the bollard. The *Centaur* eased itself a few inches away from the wall, as if eager to be gone.

Monckton's eyes were half closed.

The boy peered up, for some reason distracted by that tall, impassive figure. In a second of inattention he tripped on a sudden twist of rope and fell against the beam of the lifeboat davit, swung inboard

but loose on its pivot and ready to be turned over the starboard quarter when they had cleared the harbour entrance. The beam slashed round towards Sam. Automatically he raised his right arm; and the davit hook dug deeply into his flesh and held onto him.

Angharad cried out, sharing the agony. Monckton was already moving forward, but slowly and deliberately, seeming to time his own responses. He might almost have been prepared for such an accident.

Over his shoulder he said loudly: 'Better fetch the doctor. He's in old Mrs Wragg's on the corner.'

Odd that he should be calling in the man whose methods were the antithesis of his own — the man whom he must know had repeatedly sworn to drive him out of the village.

Caspian tensed.

Monckton was poised on the very edge of the quay, not jumping aboard but giving the appearance of reaching out prayerfully towards Sam.

Dr. Petersen came hurrying down the street, and made the leap across the

narrow gap between the quay and the barge's rail. He found time to glare at Monckton, who flicked him a strange little deferential yet gloating smile.

Sam, racked by pain, glared up too at the doctor. He saw the features blur; tried to get them in focus again.

Through Sam's eyes Caspian and Bronwen saw a shifting outline of Dr Petersen with a scalpel in his hand. The pain across Sam's eyes was as vicious as the throbbing in his arm. He struck out with his free hand, and the scalpel clattered onto the deck. Another second and Sam was brandishing it aloft.

Petersen swore, and stooped closer to get the instrument back and say something reassuring. But although his lips were moving, the syllables refused to shape themselves into sense. Every plea, every word was warped, and the man's face was warped, and behind him were not the coaming and mast and sprit and sail of the barge, but a blank white background against which Angharad's pale body began to dance a slow, lascivious dance, until Petersen was somehow entwined with her, and the two bodies and two faces were spinning in the obscene derision of Sam.

Sam got to his feet in spite of the weight of hook and davit, and used that weight and his own to drive the scalpel forward.

Angharad screamed but he did not hear her. She was not there on the quayside, but right here in front of him, dancing into a worse frenzy with the doctor.

Caspian and Bronwen tore their minds out of the thrall of Sam's delirium. They braced themselves, and plunged straight into the consciousness of the man on the edge of the quay.

Monckton was utterly stretched, concentrating every last particle of his psychic energy upon the two men struggling on deck. His own lust for Angharad added fresh contortions to the picture of her, which taunted Sam. And as Sam's rage grew, so the ideal consummation came closer: the doctor who had striven to drive Monckton out of Blackshore should be killed, and his murderer should be Sam — Sam who was also in the way, who must hang and be forever removed from the scene. In a moment it would all be over and Blackshore would be safe for Monckton and his desires.

Caspian and Bronwen struck. This had to be a mortal blow, before Sam was urged to complete his deadly task. They struck into the very core of Monckton's mind and then turned as a bayonet would turn, savaging and hacking to either side, cracking and tearing his thoughts and emotions and energies.

Monckton screamed.

The two men on the deck sprawled apart. Still Monckton fought desperately to hold Sam, forcing him to struggle up to his knees.

Then Monckton fell. Not crumpling as most men do when they collapse, but tilting slowly, rigidly forward, until he had pitched over the edge and splashed into the gap between barge and harbour wall.

A gust of wind ruffled the sea, so that the barge swung slightly. Very slightly and slowly. But implacably. Swinging inwards until the timbers caught Monckton pressed him against the unyielding stone of the wall, and went on pressing. His head was crushed in an instant.

Sam Hillaby lay quite still. A few inches away, Dr Petersen huddled for a moment over his knee, gulped in a long breath, then pushed himself upright. He sought a solution not from Sam but from Caspian and Bronwen above.

'How . . . ?' He needed another rasping breath. 'How the devil did you manage it?'

'Nothing to do with the devil,' said Caspian austerely.

'No, I'll be bound it wasn't. Except that you did defeat one, didn't you?' Petersen dragged himself up against the rail and looked over, not so much with relish as with grim acknowledgement of ultimate justice. 'I'm obliged to you Dr Caspian. And to you ma'am. The whole village ought t~ be obliged, if it has the sense to lea~ ~h,' he added with a flicker of ~ ~ristic irritability, 'I beg leave

~am he retrieved his scalpel ~ bottle of rum to splash

54

over the bloodied wound, then offered what was left to Sam so that he could take a long, numbing swallow.

'He'll be all right?' cried Angharad shakily.

'He'll be all right.' Caspian took it upon himself to comfort her.

In spite of their exhaustion, he and Bronwen summoned up the energy to venture just once more into Sam's mind. Pain twisted at it and the rum was burning his throat. But he turned to seek Angharad; and forced a shaky, loving smile.

'What's been happening here? What in the name of heaven have I been doing . . . ?'

He winced as the scalpel began to prise the hook away, then dropped through the haze of a fading dream into oblivion.

* * *

From it he would awake with one blank tract in his mind. The trouble had been eliminated and he would remember none of it. Haunted for weeks by a preordained future, which Caspian and Bronwen had ensured would not come about, he had in fact nothing to remember. Because it had not come to pass, its very possibility had ceased to be: had never been, was not, never could be.

Content, Bronwen and Caspian vacated his mind without his knowing that they had ever been in it.

Dr. Petersen nodded wryly. If there were questions, he had no intention of asking them.

A group of fishermen and the local constable advanced to the edge of the quay and peered down at the redness of a deadly rust-smeared barge and wall, seeping in long tendrils through the water, and began debating how to scoop out what was left of Healer Monckton.

THE ENTITY
STRIKES TWICE

She was away for two days and nights the first time. We called in the doctor and he shook his head and tried to look knowledgeable but it was obvious that he was baffled. His professional soothing noises did nothing to reassure us. My wife stood by the bedside crying as he trotted out his glib platitudes.

Marion lay as she always lay, her face turned up placidly towards the ceiling, her plump little mouth set in a half smile. She was anybody's dream picture of a ten-year-old daughter. But we were used to her waking up in the morning, her mouth moving, her eyes opening, the sound of a yawn and a little giggle. Now she would not wake up.

'She's breathing normally,' said the doctor. 'No tension. Nothing abnormal. Everything perfectly in order. Really' — even to himself it must have sounded absurd — 'there appears to be nothing to worry about.'

In spite of which he was worried. Not as appalled and desperate as we were, but certainly unhappy. If it went on another day, he said, he would call in a specialist or have Marion transferred to hospital for observation. He was clearly hoping that before that became necessary she would wake up and everything would be all right again.

So were we. And the third morning she did wake up, just as usual.

Well . . . not quite as usual.

Janet and I had been taking it in turns to sit by her bedside at night. We didn't want her to come to herself once more in the darkness and not know what had happened. For her sake and for our own sakes we wanted to be there when she returned to us. That morning I was dozing in the chair when the first light seeped like a slow tide into the room, gathering strength and depth, its ripples drifting across Marion's face — and across her open eyes.

I jolted upright. 'Marion . . . '

Slowly she turned her head and looked at me.

She said: 'Who are you?'

Janet must have been wide-awake in the next room. She heard our voices and in a matter of seconds she had come hurrying in.

'Is she — '

'And you,' said Marion with that particularly earnest enquiring note in her voice that we knew so well, 'who are *you?*' Then she let out a lost little whimper.

The early morning light was not as thin and cold as our fear. We looked into our daughter's eyes and met no recognition.

'Darling,' sobbed Janet, stooping over the bed.

Marion lay unresponsive for a while. Then her arms went round Janet's neck and she held on tight. One could almost feel her groping for reality. Abruptly I switched the light on, then shielded my eyes against it; and when Marion had blinked in protest and turned her head away for a few seconds, she was wide awake. She knew us again. But in the haze of waking she could not understand what the fuss was about.

'You're in here awfully early. What's the

61

matter? Daddy, what's happened?'

I said: 'You've been asleep for a long time. We've been waiting . . . '

Janet waved me surreptitiously to silence. She was right. It was best not to scare the child.

'A long time,' echoed Marion thoughtfully. Her mouth puckered. She was remembering. 'I was somewhere else.'

'You've had a horrid dream,' said Janet as firmly as she could manage. 'But it's all over now.'

'No.' Marion was careful but firm. 'It wasn't horrid. It wasn't anything. It was just living — living at home.'

We stayed with her until it was time to get up, and then Janet dressed her with shaking hands.

⋆ ⋆ ⋆

At the breakfast table, with everything safe and normal, Marion began to delve back into her dream world in spite of our attempts to keep her mind off the subject. She told us that she had been spending some time in another place. She could not describe it but it had all been very clear. It was real. She talked about it as though it might have been an hour's train journey away, beyond the city and over a hill. She had had a mother and somehow she had belonged.

But how could she have one mother there and one here?

'We do dream funny things, don't we?' said Janet, forcing a laugh.

'I felt,' said Marion, 'that I'd been living there for some time and getting used to them. In fact, I *am* used to them. And in the end I can stay there.' She dropped her spoon with a clatter and for the first time fear crept into her tale. 'But I don't want to stay there. I don't want to. It's so . . . so red there. So dried-up and so red. It hurts. It *hurts*.'

She was staring into a vision we could not see.

Janet said: 'It's all right now, darling.'

'It was a horrid dream after all. I don't belong to them, do I? Do I? I belong to you.'

'Yes, darling. You belong to us.'

'I won't ever go back there.'

'No.'

The doctor gave us a sedative for her and we kept her away from school for a week. Janet took her for little jaunts into the country. We organized life so that everything could go slowly and smoothly, allowing Marion's jumpiness and nervousness to subside. We established a slow, soothing rhythm of daily routine so that no distorted dreams would be provoked by tiredness or over-excitement.

But at the end of the week Marion went away again.

Once more she slept for two days and nights. Once more the doctor came and examined her. He found her just as before. This time he wanted to take her into hospital, but Janet refused. Marion had woken up safely the last time and there was no reason why she should not do so again. It was odd, but no more than odd: not dangerous, not worthy of hospitals and specialists and disturbing things like that.

Marion lay there as before. If she was dreaming, she gave no sign. She did not jump or writhe in her sleep and the expression of her face did not change.

When she came back, she took longer to recognize us. There was a dragging reluctance in her manner that was more alarming than her rapt sleep had been. At last she knew us, but there was no happiness in her face.

'Why did I have to come here? I don't see why it has to be me. I don't see why one of the others shouldn't come.'

After that outburst she was quiet for a long time and made no attempt to answer our tentative questions. She dressed in silence and ate most of her breakfast in silence. We tried not to stare at her and not to oppress her with our worry.

It was Janet who plunged into the disturbing lull; Janet who could not restrain herself any longer. She said:

'What was it like?'

Marion did not say a word.

'Your mother's speaking to you, Marion,' I said, sounding like every pompous parent I had ever criticized in my life.

With a politeness that was forced yet impeccable, Marion replied, 'Oh. I'm sorry. What did you say?'

'Darling, I just wondered what it was like. This dream of yours — the place in it.'

'You can't say 'was'. The place *is*. And everybody in it: And it isn't just a dream.'

Janet opened her mouth and I could see she was going to say something sharp. She was upset, teetering on the verge of tears. I wanted to keep it calm and reasonable until Marion was herself again. I broke in quickly.

'You haven't told us exactly what it's like.'

Marion deliberated for a moment as though wondering whether it was really worth her while to tell us. Then she said in a casual way that was older than her years:

'It's a town. A white town where there's no dirt and no noise. And,' she added with a strange sidelong glance at Janet, 'no fools. We all know one another and we're all part of the same . . . the same life.'

'What do you mean?' I asked.

'You wouldn't understand. It would

66

take too long to explain, even though on the surface there are no obvious differences. There are families just as here, but they all combine to make up a larger family. There are no inadequacies of communication and no fundamental misunderstandings . . . '

She went on lucidly and coherently, yet I could make no sense out of what she was saying. I was startled by the phrases she used. She had an adult personality and vocabulary. She described — or, rather, tried to describe — a community that sounded more like a philosophical nirvana than a collection of human beings, and I could not imagine where she got her ideas from. Even in a dream a child could hardly reach so far out beyond her own personal experience. Marion was a gay, bouncy little girl who didn't spell terribly well and didn't make much of a hit at school and had difficulty with long words. This was not like her.

I found that I was hardly listening after the first few minutes. I was too busily occupied with trying to hold on to the idea of Marion — of Marion herself.

There seemed to be two of her now: one our own Marion, trying to explain things to herself as much as to us, and the other a separate being who put words in her mouth or, every now and then, snatched them away and slyly diverted her.

'And outside the town,' she concluded, 'there's what is left. Not like here.' Her gaze went past us, out towards the garden and the brief slope of the field behind it. 'It's so green here,' she said. 'So horribly green. It hurts.' She put her hand over her eyes. 'I've got to get used to it. We've all got to get used to it. But it hurts.'

We debated whether or not to keep her away from school again. It had done little good the last time. Perhaps the safest course was to let her mix with her friends and get caught up again in the everyday ritual of school and lessons.

It appeared to work out. She went off at the usual time, and came back at the usual time. She was not quite the chatterbox we were accustomed to, and did not babble on about the misdeeds of her friends and enemies in the familiar way; nor did she complain. Janet and I asked her no questions, we asked ourselves few questions. In a way we were holding our breath, not wanting to admit that anything was seriously wrong. Leave her alone and she'll be all right — that was what we silently assured ourselves.

In the middle of the week I met her teacher outside the public library. Miss Rossiter was a stringy spinster with a severe manner and a deep, complex affection for her pupils. As soon as she saw me she came loping along the pavement with one arm raised in a characteristically declamatory gesture.

'Mr Seddon, I'm so glad to see you. I've been meaning to send a note home with Marion, but you know how rushed one is.'

'Nothing wrong, I hope?'

'Well . . . '

'Come on, Miss Rossiter,' I coaxed her. 'We're not difficult parents. You ought to know that by now.'

She flushed. 'Of course I know it, Mr Seddon. It's not that at all. It's simply that I am not sure how to put the matter into words.'

'Has Marion been behaving at all oddly?' I tried to make it sound light and unconcerned, while I waited to hear the worst.

'Oddly, yes. Did you know she had quarrelled with Penny?'

This I didn't know. Penny was the daughter of our next-door neighbours, and she and Marion had been inseparable friends for five or six years. They had their inevitable bickerings, but nothing had ever really shaken their friendship,

I said uncertainly, 'They'll get over it.'

'Indeed I hope so. But it has all been rather disturbing. I don't know the source of the disagreement, but I have observed that Marion now regards little Penny with out-and-out contempt. She literally looks down on her — and, I'm afraid, on a lot of others in the class. At present she appears to be making friends with a girl called Lucille Banks in the next class.'

This was surprising. I knew the Banks girl. She lived round the corner from us, and quite apart from being older and a lot cleverer than Marion she had always struck me as being a quite antipathetic type. When the two girls passed in the street you felt a sort of internal snarl, like two dogs bristling at each other. That they should have struck up a friendship was unsettling.

'Also,' went on Miss Rossiter, 'I'm at a loss to account for Marion's sudden progress in class. What did you do with her that week she was away — cram her with maths?'

'She did no work at all,' I said. 'She was resting.'

'Then I simply do not understand. She is now not only the most brilliant child in my class, but may well be one of the most brilliant in the school. Within a few days I have been convinced of this. She's incredible. Mr. Seddon, what has happened to the child?'

What, indeed, had happened to our child?

*   *   *

Janet reported trouble. After I had told her about the split between Marion and Penny she had tried to dig the truth out

71

of Marion. She had been slapped down for her pains. It was none of her business; she couldn't be expected to understand, that had been Marion's derisive attitude. The child had treated her mother like dirt. 'I've no time for simpletons,' she had declared, and it had been difficult to decide whether she was referring to her mother or to Penny.

That night in her room I talked to Marion myself. From the way she glared at me I knew that Janet had not been exaggerating.

I said: 'Why do you hate us?'

'We don't hate you.'

'Who do you mean by 'we'?'

'It would be a waste of time trying to explain.' A complete stranger was talking to me and looking at me.

'Marion, what's got into you?'

'Into me?' The concept seemed to amuse her.

And undoubtedly there was somebody else within her. Somebody else was studying me through her eyes and gradually taking her over, taking on a new strength and character.

As though she could read my mind she said: 'When I come back I'll be stronger.'

Before I could press her any further she turned over and went off to sleep immediately.

She was late waking up in the morning, and we thought she would once again be away for a couple of days. This time we began seriously to consider the idea of sending her to hospital. We discussed it in undertones as though afraid of waking her.

'I know it's an awful thing to say,' Janet murmured shakily, 'but . . . oh, I almost wish . . . I don't know that I want her to come back. Not the way she has been, I don't think she ought to come back. I'm scared.'

We quarrelled, still not raising our voices. I accused her of callousness and of having some psychological kink, even though I knew it to be untrue. I vented my own unease on her and she spat back at me. Perhaps it helped to relieve our feelings. We were both exhausted by the long controlled, suppressed outburst.

There was no telling when Marion

woke up. She might have been awake for a long time, listening to us. If so, she showed no sign of being upset. We simply became aware that her eyes were open.

She got up silently and began to dress herself.

Janet cried, 'You've been away again, haven't you?'

'Yes,' said Marion indifferently.

My wife clutched my arm. I wanted to order her not to start a row all over again and not to alarm Marion, but that would have been absurd. Nothing now would alarm Marion. She was in complete possession of herself — or perhaps it was more accurate to say that she was now completely possessed.

'Where is she?' sobbed Janet. 'Where is Marion?'

'Somewhere else,' came the placid reply.

'Why? And who are you?'

'You wouldn't understand.' It was the same, repetitive response. 'This is the only way across. It has taken us a long time to find it — a long time to build up the strength — but we are here now. And we stay here.'

'Marion — '

'She's happy enough. She'll be all right for the rest of her life — short as it's likely to be.'

'What do you mean by that?' I demanded.

'There's not much left over there. Not much food, not much air. Not much time.' Her eyes narrowed with pain. 'We've got to start moving the older ones across soon. It will be easier for them now that we know how. It's not that we want to come here. Not to this dull planet, back to primeval conditions. But it has a long way to go — and ours hasn't.'

Janet said again, faintly: 'Marion.'

'It will be short,' said the child impassively, 'and painless for her.'

She got ready for school. As she was in the hall putting her hat on, Janet said urgently to me: 'She's got to be stopped. Before . . . '

'Before what?'

'I don't know. But we've got to act, Alan.'

Marion appeared in the doorway and looked from one to the other of us. It would not be true to say that she appeared scary: she was too utterly removed even for that.

We watched her go. She did not offer to kiss us, and did not look back as she went down the path to the front gate.

That night when I came home it was to find that Janet had killed her.

* * *

Marion's arrogance had increased by the time she got back from school, as though feeding on the inferiority of her class-mates. She had made only the sketchiest of attempts to be polite to her mother. Janet, her nerves on edge, had spoken to her as most distraught mothers speak to their children from time to time, finishing up with the familiar shout: 'Do you know who you're talking to?'

'Yes,' Marion had replied insolently. 'But *you* don't know who *you're* talking to.'

She had then gone upstairs to her room, dismissing the whole thing. Janet had raced upstairs in pursuit. They had stood on the landing, Janet screaming at her, and Marion had coldly flailed her with humiliating contempt. At last Janet had hit her. And Marion hissed, 'Scum.'

Janet reached for the first thing that came to hand. It was a small but heavy wooden statue of a grinning animal, which I had brought back from Burma years ago and which had stood on the landing window ledge. Janet slammed it twice against Marion's head, and Marion staggered for a long moment and then fell down the stairs. She was dead when she reached the bottom.

Janet was sitting in a terrible stupor when I reached home. I left her while I had a look at Marion, and then I went away and was sick. When I had washed my face and had a drink and stopped trembling, I took the statue and looked despairingly around. We had no open fireplace, and I couldn't risk putting it in the dustbin. Right now it was just a matter of getting it out of the way. I couldn't bear to wash it — couldn't bear to wipe Marion's matted blood off it. I took it up into the attic and stowed it away behind the cistern for the time being, and then came down and tried to get Janet into some sort of shape before we called in the doctor and the police.

It was an accident, of course. I did all the talking. They were all very sympathetic towards Janet, and she managed to confirm that she had seen Marion falling downstairs. The doctor told of the child's two inexplicable bouts of unconsciousness, and gave his opinion that she must have been overtaken by a dizzy spell in some way connected with the illness. She had struck her head against the stairs and the wall on the way down. That was how she died.

After it was over I had the task of shielding and comforting Janet. She was in danger of a breakdown. She began to reproach herself bitterly. It was too easy to forget what Marion had been like these past few weeks and to remember how adorable she had been before that time. Janet felt that somehow, in some way she could not comprehend, the whole thing must have been her fault.

I did all I could, but deep down I knew

that the dark shadow could never be driven out of the house.

Little Penny next door was heartbroken. She, too, remembered only the good things about Marion and forgot their recent quarrel.

Lucille Banks was a different matter.

I passed her on the corner of the street one evening and she looked straight at me. Just looked, said nothing. It was like being struck across the face. In her eyes was the same expression I had seen in Marion's after she had ceased to be Marion. I got the impression that she was waiting, but waiting for what?

★ ★ ★

Janet began to dream.

One morning she told me incoherently that she had seen Marion again — *our* Marion.

'She's still there. She hasn't changed. She was so glad to see me, so . . . oh, Alan, if you knew . . . It's so red over there. It hurts. But she's Marion, and we were talking, and . . . oh, why did I have to wake up?'

I didn't go to the office that day. I stayed at home and tried to dig out of Janet what she had seen. But like any dream, by the middle of the morning it had faded, and after a while she grew impatient at my questions. She didn't want to talk. She wanted to be left in the sombre silence of her remote thoughts.

That night she dreamed of Marion again. She told me so, but would not go into detail.

I wanted to shake her out of this mood but dared not be too brusque. The death of Marion would prey on her mind for years — perhaps forever — and she must be treated carefully. Apparent normality was important. The next day I went back to the office, once more with the belief that had proved so foolish in Marion's case — the belief that if you pretend everything is normal it will somehow become so of its own accord.

In the evening my slippers had been put in their usual place. Janet cooked an excellent dinner, and though we ate without saying very much I began to feel that things weren't too bad, that it was all going to come right. We watched television, and when Janet suggested that we went to bed early there was a note of appeal in her voice, revealing that she was anxious to get back to her dreams; I didn't let myself hear it.

When I tried to put my arms round her in bed she moved instinctively away. I felt that there was a great distance between us. Long after she had gone to sleep I lay awake and wondered apprehensively if we were going to drift further apart and if she was going to retreat further into herself and hide away from me and the rest of the world.

Gradually tiredness claimed me. I hung for a long time between the drowsy reality of our bedroom and the soothing slumber of forgetfulness. Finally I relaxed my grip and slid down into the shadows.

And the shadows began to move and to take on a life of their own.

First of all there were strange white shapes jutting up at irrational angles through a red haze that refused to clear. I stumbled among them, and as I went on they grew firmer in outline, though still obscured by the swirling dust.

Somebody spoke to me in a language which I had never heard before yet which was on the verge of making sense.

I knew that I was being drawn on and that after a while I would find myself in a place more solid and more comprehensible. At once I stopped. Something in my nature refused to be coaxed in this way. I wasn't going to be lured on. I wasn't going to give up, wasn't going to let the very essence of my being suffer the strange distillation that was being prepared for it.

There was anger in the air. They were not used to being thwarted. In some way which I could not explain, I knew that they had not encountered resistance before, and their response was an immediate viciousness. Some force slammed into my mind as though to throw it off balance. Like a patient resisting hypnosis, I fought back — and it was like clambering up out of a morass, finding solid ground here and there and gradually emerging into safety.

I awoke, and it was morning. Janet lay staring at the ceiling. I said: 'Have you been having any dreams?'

'Dreams?' she said blandly. 'No, not a thing.'

I was chilled by the fixed, almost mocking self-assurance of her gaze as she sat up and looked down on me.

Her expression remained like a taunting ghost in my mind all the time I was in the office. Occasionally it blurred and mingled with other ghosts — tantalising shapes from nightmare, sometimes seeming to offer vague promises and at other times uttering threats.

I tried to pull myself together. At this rate my work was going to suffer and that would do nobody any good. The business of living had to go on.

I passed Lucille Banks again on my way home. She watched me all the way along the street until I reached my own front door. I was glad to get inside and close it behind me.

Janet did not come out into the hall to meet me. It was not until I had hung up my coat and walked into the sitting room that I found we had visitors. The police were waiting for me.

★ ★ ★

They were very polite but very bleak. They asked their questions as though they knew all the answers and required from me only formal confirmation. Janet sat with her head bowed, apparently not listening, yet hearing every word that was said.

The bloodstained statue sat on a clean handkerchief in the middle of the coffee table. It looked squat and evil, like some obscene animal god sated with sacrifice. But I mustn't let myself be caught up in such fancies. It was nothing but a heavy piece of carved wood which my wife had hysterically slammed against our daughter's head.

The police inspector said: 'It would appear, then, that your daughter did not in fact fall downstairs as you claimed. Before falling she was brutally struck with that object, struck with intent to murder.'

I could not answer. I stared at him and

then at Janet. Her head was still lowered.

'Having killed her,' the inspector continued, 'you were clear-headed enough to make immediate arrangements to hide the instrument of death. Not until it was safely tucked away in the attic did you send for the doctor and the police.'

I wondered desperately how they had found the statue and why they should have been looking for it in the first place. Even if I knew the answer, it wasn't going to help. The evidence was here. There was no concealing it now.

The inspector asked, 'Don't you think you'd better tell the truth, sir?' Before I could grope for some sense in all this, he added formally, 'I must warn you, of course, that anything you say may be taken down and used in evidence.'

Tell the truth . . . and implicate Janet. It was unthinkable. Yet what was the alternative?

At last Janet raised her head. She was going to speak. I wanted to shout at her, to stop her; to tell her not to incriminate herself, to give me time to sort it out.

Then I saw her face and I was struck dumb.

'Alan,' she said very softly, 'don't you think it's better this way? I can't go on covering up for you for the rest of our life. I can't stand it. I'm sorry, Alan, but it won't work.'

Her voice was gentle and persuasive, full of calculated affection. It was most convincing. But the satisfaction in her eyes was a negation of every word she uttered.

I need have no compunction. This was no longer my wife. Janet had gone, just as Marion had gone. I sensed that she would never come back. She had been . . . *replaced*. She was a mere mask of her former self, nothing but a controlled medium. And she and her people, whoever they were, must not get away with this.

I said: 'You're on the wrong track, Inspector. I admit I concealed evidence, but there were reasons. Now those reasons no longer apply. It was my wife who killed Marion. You will find her fingerprints on that statue.'

He looked at me with undisguised loathing. When he spoke, he snapped the words out as though anxious to hurl them in my face. 'Your wife's fingerprints are on the statue,' he conceded. 'Hardly surprising, since it was she who carried it downstairs before telephoning us and telling us the story of what really happened. But they are not as marked as your fingerprints.'

I remembered how tautly I had gripped the thing as I carried it up to the attic, holding onto it with all the force of my mounting terror at the time.

'And,' the inspector went on remorselessly, 'if you are thinking that a wife cannot give testimony against her husband, or that you might try to swing the blame onto her and fig the issue in court, I have to inform you that she is not the only witness. One of your daughter's school friends was in the house at the time, watching. You didn't know that, did you, Mr. Seddon? It was she who persuaded your wife that the truth must be told.'

'Who was it?' I asked, although I

already knew the answer.

'It was Lucille,' Janet confirmed. 'I didn't tell you that, Alan, because I was so scared. She had been here playing with Marion, and when you came home she hid, intending to get out of the house without meeting you. She was frightened of you — as we all were.'

'But why?' I burst out, unable to hold it in any longer. 'Why frame me like this? If you . . . people hate Marion's murderer, you know as well as I do that it wasn't me. Why pick on me?'

'Alan,' said Janet in that same hurt, persuasive voice, 'you're resisting the truth. You've always resisted it. And it's no good.'

The police inspector nodded solemnly. But he didn't know what she was talking about. *I* was the only one who understood what she meant.

They had given me the opportunity. They had contacted me and I had rejected them. I wasn't susceptible; they couldn't come in through me. I was a potential danger to them, living with Janet; beginning, perhaps, to understand more and more of what was going on and in the end perhaps being able to warn others. There were bound to be casualties, as there had been with Marion; but they could forgive that, if Marion's killer could herself be converted in the end to their own purposes. For me there was no chance.

And nobody in this world would now believe a word that I spoke.

* * *

Nobody does believe. The evidence has been piled up against me and my defence is regarded as a cunning attempt to establish insanity as an excuse.

Lucille Banks made a good showing in court. She was so obviously an honest little girl, so obviously fond of her dead school friend. She lied so admirably about the stories Marion told her about me — the brutal father of whom she was so afraid, of whom her mother was so afraid. And Lucille had hidden, shivering, under the stairs when I came in, and had heard me yelling at Marion and then attacking her. Lucille . . . who never once set foot in our house until she came back to work out her nefarious plans with Janet.

There was not much hope from the start. And when I looked along the jury and found there three faces that were the same as Janet's, the same as Lucille's, the same as Marion's had been, I knew I was finished. There were nine people on that jury who didn't believe my story, and three who did, but their verdict came to the same thing.

They have decided to execute me, though I hear that there is a movement afoot to ask for a reprieve. Some people think I am genuinely insane, and even if I'm not they favour a life sentence rather than a death sentence. For myself, I favour the swift dark. If I were to linger on I would always be yearning for those others, those people from the other side — wherever it may be — to contact me again. And I don't think they intend to. If they did, I might still not be able to give in to them. Unlike Janet, who succumbed so easily and smoothly because part of her longed to see Marion again and was willing to sacrifice everything to accomplish that, I know I would fight against being taken over. Even when I wanted to go, I would stay stubbornly here.

For the sake of the human race I hope there are others like me. I hope there will be enough resolute, dogged men and women to hold out against the invasion.

And as for Janet and Marion . . . for them I hope that there is happiness in being together. Wherever they may be, and however short their time is in that red, alien world to which they have been banished, at least they are together and the pain will not be too terrible.

I wish I could be with them.

THE DEVIL'S TRITONE

The Orkney wind had caused the postponement of one concert during the St. Magnus Festival because a small circular window had been blown out of the cathedral by the force of the gale. A less exposed recital given by the Drysdale Trio on Shapinsay started late because of the ferry's slow struggle across the short but turbulent stretch between Kirkwall and the island. But the recital had been a success. People who had taken that much trouble to get there in such weather conditions were determined to enjoy the music, even when one banshee wail of a more ferocious gust howled in quite the wrong key.

This came in the middle of *Variations on a Theme by Calum of the Clachan,* which Robert Drysdale had composed for the three of them — himself on violin, his wife Deirdre on the clarsach, and their daughter Fiona on flute. Somehow, although it produced such a grinding discord, the cry of the wind seemed an integral part of the work, producing a shiver for which the strange convolutions of the melody had been preparing the listener.

The day after the final concert, the ferry to the mainland ran four hours late because of the fury of the wind along the Pentland Firth. The Drysdales had never been seasick, but by the time Robert drove off the ramp on to solid ground he was still dizzy from bracing himself against the lurching and plunging of the vessel. Half a mile clear of the ferry terminal, he drew in to the side of the road.

'We'll have to find somewhere else to spend the night. It's too late to make Pitlochry by this evening.'

They were due to play another recital in Hexham in Northumberland two days from now. He had planned to break the journey a good way down central Scotland, and then have plenty of time next day for a leisurely drive south of the Border.

Deirdre reached for the map and opened it across her lap. 'Dornoch?' she suggested.

'Or a bit further inland. We could make Bonar Bridge, or . . . just a minute.' Robert's finger jabbed at a name. 'Kirkshiel. Only a few miles off the direct route. And couldn't be more appropriate.'

'Why's that?'

'Calum of the Clachan, that's why. That's where he came from, and where he went back to in the end.'

'I didn't think there ever was a place with a real name,' said Fiona from the back seat. 'Didn't he call himself 'of the Clachan' because his home village was abandoned during the Clearances and never had a real name of its own?'

As the wind buffeted the side of the Volvo, Robert thought of the wind of cruelty that had swept across the Highlands when rapacious landlords and their factors drove men off the land to make room for sheep. Some emigrated, while others were resettled into jobs on the bleak coast, which was utterly alien to them. Others, like Calum of the Clachan, wandered — an itinerant fiddler, literally scraping a living as he travelled.

Robert glanced at his wife. 'You ought to feel in tune with the man. Your own ancestors did enough stravaiging in their time.'

Deirdre laughed gently, as if dissociating herself from those wandering clarsairs from Eriskay who had carried their harps and their music from one glen to another, one misty hill to another, across land and water, one island to another.

'And he did find his way home in the end,' Robert added.

There must have been a few gradual resettlements when the railway came reasonably close on its way up through Lairg. Kirkshiel was one of them: still pretty small, but at least there was an inn marked on the map. It was worth a try.

Robert drove beside the twists and turns of a winding river. Passing places were marked with triangular signs. During the first hour, they met only one caravan bumping along the road towards some hidden caravan park, or perhaps simply seeking a patch in the trees beside the road.

Fiona began humming to herself. Robert, usually relaxed when he was driving and rarely distracted by irritating sounds, human or mechanical, paid no attention at first. Then the sound became a nagging nuisance, plucking at his mind with thorny insistence.

'What on earth's that you're droning away at?'

'I don't know. It just came into my head.'

Fiona fell silent; but as they approached Kirkshiel she said: 'That tune. It's getting louder in my head.'

At this time of year in the northern isles and on the northern mainland there were little more than a couple of hours of near-darkness. But although the sun was still coating the treetops with a burnished glow, the sky ahead was sullen and threatening thunder. The wind had dropped, leaving a muggy stillness. Robert drove round a sharp bend, and the road began dipping towards a small settlement with a few lights in windows here and there.

The inn was called The Crofter's Rest. One of its windows was brighter than any of its neighbours.

Robert left the women in the Volvo and went into the bar. It was a long, low room with four stools, a high-backed trestle against the window, and two tables at the far end. A fruit machine blinked with a migraine-inducing dazzle in an alcove near the door to the toilets.

The landlord, in shirtsleeves, was resting his bony elbows on the bar, his rheumy eyes sizing up the newcomer without bothering to offer any greeting. His forearms were mottled with purple blotches, and his greying hair looked dusty rather than potentially silver.

'Could you manage accommodation for three of us?' asked Robert. 'Just for one night?'

'Three of you?'

'My wife and myself, and a room for my daughter.'

'Aye.' The landlord seemed neither welcoming nor reluctant. 'And you'd be wanting to eat?'

'If you can rustle something up, that would be great.'

'We're well stocked. Ready for tomorrow evening.'

'You've got a function on? A party?'

'An annual event, aye.'

When Robert went out to tell the women that they could come indoors, the landlord followed, not offering help with the two cases but peering with shameless curiosity at the instruments in the back of the estate wagon.

'Ye'd be musicians, then?'

'Just been to the St. Magnus Festival in Orkney. Oddly enough,' said Robert as he heaved one of the cases out, 'we recently played some variations on a tune by one of your local characters — Calum of the Clachan.'

'Just the right folk for tomorrow evening, then.'

'Sorry?'

'Calum's Night, we call it. Once a year. Just the once. And there's need of music. The right kind o' music.'

'I'm afraid we won't be here tomorrow evening.'

'Now, that would be a pity. A great pity, since you've been sent here.'

'Hardly. We just happened to notice the name on the map, and — '

'Well, let's say you were drawn here, then.'

They were shown up a narrow flight of stairs to a cramped landing with two bedrooms and a bathroom opening off it. The ceilings were low, and the rooms were dark, each with only one small dormer window, but they were spotlessly clean, and there was a fresh smell from the bed linen.

As they unpacked, Deirdre said abruptly: 'I think perhaps we ought to have driven on.'

'Whatever for? This looks comfortable enough. Nice and quiet.'

'There's something . . . waiting.'

Robert put his arm round her. 'Come on, now. Don't go all fey on us.'

She turned away and began hanging two dresses in the narrow wardrobe.

When they went down, the landlord this time came along the bar to greet them. 'Ready for a drink, now, sir?' He sounded almost pleased that they were here. 'I'm Hamish. Hamish McReay.'

'Drysdale. My wife Deirdre, our daughter Fiona.'

Hamish nodded as if to grant this his approval, and when he had poured a pint of rather gassy beer and two orange-and-lemonades for them, he said: 'Would trout or steak be what you'd be wanting for your meal?'

'Trout,' said Deirdre and Fiona almost in chorus.

'Steak,' said Robert.

They perched on the bar stools while Hamish went through a door with their order. When he came back, he seemed to have mellowed a fraction further and was ready to play the talkative host.

'Tomorrow evening, now. We've been let down by one of our locals. He's been training up for it since last year. But he . . . och, he wasnae up to it. Ran off at the last minute.'

'Stage fright?'

'Been put off by silly tales. And some of those so-called professionals have been no better. There was one of those pop groups came here, talking big. Called themselves The Sons of the Gael, or some such thing. Pop music and what they said was traditional folk music. Or folk rock, or whatever name they chose to put on it. Some o' the younger folk liked them. They played what they called a gig on Calum's Night. The fiddler took some holding back that night, I'll grant ye. Said he'd be back the next year, but he never came. Quite a few like that. Say they'll come back, but they don't. And then we hear, every now and then, of some of them dying.'

'These folk-pop groups.' Robert sympathized. 'All the same. Get high on the music and on drugs at the same time, and kill themselves with it.'

'Aye,' said Hamish without seeming quite to accept this. 'It could be that, maybe.'

'But this annual do — what's it all about?'

'Calum's Night, as I told ye. Every year there's a celebration. Some music, some dancing.'

'What a coincidence, us being here so close to it.'

'Och, no. That'll no' be a coincidence. It was meant. You being here, that is.'

'But I've told you, we've got to be on

104

our way tomorrow. We can't help out.'

Hamish smiled with the infuriating smugness of someone who thought he knew better, and went to serve two young men who had just come in and propped themselves against the far end of the bar. Dark and almost gypsyish, they muttered between themselves, grinned, and stared at the strangers. Particularly at Fiona, with her red hair, redder than her mother's, in a tight casque over her head, with a little stub at the back like a seaman's tobacco quid.

Looking away, Fiona reached for a leaflet from a plastic container propped against an upright beam. Robert leaned over her shoulder as she opened the creased, faded pages. As a tourist pamphlet it was far from inspiring, listing a few fishing rights, a two-mile walk, and remains of a prehistoric stone circle.

'And no mention of their prodigal son?'

'Not a word.'

Hamish lifted a flap to allow an elderly woman through, carrying two large plates which she put down on one of the tables. As they settled themselves around the table, she was on her way back to fetch a tray bearing another plate and a bowl of vegetables.

Fiona slid the leaflet back onto the bar.

'You'd have expected at least some mention of Calum of the Clachan. At least a couple of lines. I wonder if there's a plaque or a sign somewhere in the village?'

'Those who know,' said the woman at her left shoulder, leaning over to put servers in the vegetable bowl, 'hae no need of it.'

'And those who don't know?' laughed Fiona.

'Are gey better without it.'

Hamish cleared his throat with a warning growl, and the woman scuttled away. The young men finished their drinks and left, with a last glance at Fiona. Hamish sauntered along to lean on the counter above the Drysdales.

'Quiet tonight,' said Deirdre politely, between mouthfuls.

'Saving themselves for tomorrow,' said Hamish, 'as ye'll see.'

Robert clattered his knife down on the

plate. 'Mr. McReay, I've already told you, we'll be off in the morning. We definitely won't be here tomorrow evening.'

'It'd be a great shame for you to miss it. Wouldnae be right at all.'

★　★　★

Robert spent a restless night. He felt that he had still not got his land legs back. The bed was swaying as if he were still aboard the ferry. Beside him, Deirdre was quite still and said nothing; but he knew that she was awake most of the night.

In the morning they were offered a large breakfast.

'Should see us most of the way,' said Fiona.

The old woman said not a word, but made an odd little chuckling sound with her tongue against her teeth.

When Robert went to pay the bill, Hamish McReay hummed and hawed, and regretted that he had no way of coping with a credit card. When Robert took out his cheque book, Hamish agreed that yes, that would be all right.

'But why not wait till tomorrow morning? I'm thinking that then we might offer ye the two nights free of charge.'

'But that's ridiculous.'

'We'd be greatly beholden to ye.'

'I'm afraid we have to be on our way. Right now.'

Hamish took the cheque but pushed it away from him along the bar as if not taking it seriously. He made no effort to help Robert and Fiona as they took their two cases out to the car, but stood in the doorway of the inn watching them sceptically.

They settled themselves into their usual positions in the car, and Robert put the key into the ignition automatically, as he had done a thousand times before.

There was no response. Not a whisper from the engine.

The car refused to start.

Robert swore, and tried again. At last he got out and lifted the bonnet. Oil, water, points, fuses: everything seemed normal. After twenty frustrating minutes, he dug his mobile phone out and brought up the breakdown service number.

There was no response from the phone, either. They must be in a dead spot.

Resentfully Robert strode back to the inn, where Hamish was still standing in the doorway.

'May I use your phone?'

Hamish stood aside and waved his hand towards a shelf within a cramped alcove.

A cheerful voice took Robert's policy number and said, even more cheerfully, that there might be a slight delay because of his distance from one of their contract garages, but somebody would be on his way as soon as possible.

Robert stormed back to the car. He was damned if they would go back and wait in the inn, with Hamish McReay smirking at their discomfiture. Rather than that, they could fill in time by going to see where Calum lay. A hundred yards down the hill Robert could see the little church, and it would obviously be possible from there to see when the breakdown man arrived at the inn.

'Since we've got to fill in the time,' he snapped, 'let's go and visit the bloody man who brought us here.'

They walked down to the squat little building, with its one tiny bell in its small cage on the roof. It might have been a scaled-down replica of one of Telford's austere 'Parliamentary' churches. There was a scattering of graves in the church-yard, with a few little pots of fresh flowers in front of the headstones, and grass that had been neatly trimmed. Robert checked that they could indeed see the Volvo from here, and then tried the church door. It squeaked open, and they went in.

The interior was cold in spite of the warmth of the morning outside. The walls were a plain, chill white, the backs of the pews stiffly upright. A board displayed lopsided numbers of last week's hymns. Against the north wall was what looked like a small stone coffin, with a child's name and date of death on it. Facing it from the south wall was a larger tomb, but this one was incongruously in heavy wood, pockmarked with knots.

The three of them stared down at the faded paint that formed a succession of red and green stripes across the lid, like a crude representation of straps holding a cabin trunk together.

Behind them a peevish, reedy voice said: 'I suppose you've come for a cheap thrill?'

The minister was a short man with narrow shoulders and a narrow face. His pursed lips were tightening as if to deliver a bitter sermon right here and now.

'Our car has broken down,' said Robert, 'and we're stuck here until someone comes to fix it. We're simply filling in time.'

'Hm. You know this accursed man's reputation?'

'We know his music. Actually, we've played some of it. Variations on one of his fiddle themes.'

'May God forgive you.' The minister's sallow cheeks were puckered with loathing as he stared at the strange wooden sarcophagus. 'The creature should never have been laid to rest here. If he does rest.' He drew a deep, shuddering breath. 'Like his devilish master, he should have been forbidden the solace of a consecrated place.'

111

'His master?' whispered Fiona, puzzled.

'The devil Paganini. A wanderer himself — a poisonous visitor to Scotland in the 1830s, making hideous discord in his music across the land and in the minds of his listeners.'

'Paganini did develop some rather startling harmonics in his playing,' Robert agreed, 'but nowadays we take them for granted, and — '

'We take too many evils for granted. And allow too many disciples of the Devil to indulge in their wicked orgies.'

'Even Paganini was forgiven in the end and duly reburied in — '

'Forgiven by his acolytes, themselves the servants of evil. But Calum of the Clachan was never known even to *seek* forgiveness. He lived only for his music. Or one might say he lived on it. Wandering from shameless town to innocent village, indulging in his wild flights, urging people on to dance themselves into perdition. They speak of at least three women who danced themselves to death — and he fed on them. His music fed on them, and kept him alive.'

'I take it,' said Robert sardonically, 'that you won't be having any performances in the church here, in connection with Calum's Night?'

'I'll have no such blasphemy in this place.' The minister glanced apprehensively at the wooden tomb. 'I would never risk letting them get so . . . so close. You ought not to be so close if you've come to take part in their obscenities.'

'We came only out of curiosity, and to find a bed for the night.' It must, thought Robert, be awkward for the minister of a parish as small and inbred as this to be at odds with the locals. 'Look,' he ventured, 'if you disapprove so strongly of their little annual festivity, aren't you in a position to condemn it from your pulpit?'

'I have learned to turn a blind eye and a deaf ear to what goes on just this one night of the year.' The reediness of the priest's voice became a shrill lament. 'All the rest of the year, they come to church meekly enough. Just that there's the one night a year, one night in honour of . . . ' He stopped, his breathing shaking his body. 'Nay, in dishonour . . . ' He held out shaking hands towards the woodwork but did not touch it. 'Something evil has for too long infested that box. Gone on living when it ought to have died long ago.'

'You don't really believe in — '

'I pray to believe only in what is right.' The minister was visibly trying to control himself. 'You say you are musicians. And you will be playing for him tonight?'

'Certainly not. We've got bogged down for an hour or two, but — '

'You have let yourself be trapped.' Walking away the priest turned at the doorway. 'I shall pray for you.' He did not sound optimistic.

★   ★   ★

They walked back up the slope and reluctantly went back into the inn, where the old woman served them coffee and biscuits while Hamish McReay polished the bar counter and checked his pumps at a self-satisfied, leisurely pace.

'This isn't good enough. What do we pay these breakdown people for?' Robert drained his coffee and went to the phone again.

This time the response was less cheerful. There had been an unusual number of accidents that morning, and the garage nearest to Kirkshiel had had trouble with their breakdown vehicle. 'And' — the voice grew wary and uncomfortable — 'one of the men there says something about not fancying anything in Kirkshiel today. Tomorrow should be all right, but today . . . well, there's something about it that people round there don't fancy.'

'This is ridiculous. The weather's perfectly reasonable. No problems. Can't you call somebody else in?'

'I've done my best. But there's just something odd about that place. I do assure you that we'll have organized something by tomorrow.'

Fiona and Deirdre looked up at Robert as he came back. Even without uttering a single question their faces were as unoptimistic as the minister's had been.

'Tomorrow!' Robert raged. 'Everything can be fixed tomorrow, but for some bloody stupid reason not today.'

'Your car will start in the morning.' Hamish was beginning to polish an array of glasses. 'Have nae fear. And now' — he puffed breath onto a glass and rubbed away — 'ye'll have to stay another night. Now ye'll be playing for Calum's Night. Which is as it should be.'

'I've a damn good mind to start walking. It can't be that many miles to — '

'Daddy,' said Fiona very quietly, 'I don't think they'd let us.'

'What d'you mean? Who's to stop us?'

'In any case,' said Deirdre, 'we're not going to walk away and leave our instruments. Not even just to go for a stroll.'

'Your car will start in the morning,' said Hamish again.

There was nothing for it. With a bad grace Robert accepted that they would have to eat lunch here, and somehow pass away the hours of the afternoon. And then?

It was an excellent lunch, but he had difficulty in forcing down each mouthful.

His wife and daughter ate slowly, but seemed to appreciate the food. As they were finishing, Deirdre said:

'We can't just sit here and sulk. And somehow I don't fancy an afternoon nap.'

'I wouldn't sleep a wink,' Robert agreed ruefully.

'So why don't we bring the instruments in, and rehearse? We're not going to have as much time as we'd like when we do reach Hexham, so why not practise now?'

In such surroundings, and in such a situation, Robert felt in no mood to tackle the music he loved. But Deirdre was right. Practising would soon draw them in, and would do them good.

They brought the violin, the clarsach and the flute in. Still wearing that infuriatingly complacent grin, Hamish McReay was holding open a door, which led to the back of the inn. Here they found a room more spacious than the general layout of the inn would have led one to guess at. At one end was a small, shallow platform with three chairs already in place.

Deirdre had been right. Within fifteen

minutes they were absorbed in the problems and nuances of the programme that they had planned for Hexham. With one exception. There was an instinctive unspoken agreement between them that the *Variations on a Theme by Calum of the Clachan* should not be played this afternoon.

When they stopped, Hamish was ready with a beer and the orange-and-lemonade that the women fancied, and which they needed after their exertions.

'And ye'll be glad of a wee rest before the commemoration begins.'

'Look, after all this, you don't imagine we're going to be forced into playing at this shindig of yours?'

'What else would ye be doing with your evening?'

'Damnit, I won't be pressured.'

Deirdre was beside him, speaking close to his left ear. 'Robert my love, it's too late. We should never have come here. But now we're here, we have to go through with this.'

People began gathering early in the evening. At first they might have been no more than regulars dropping in for a dram on their way home from work. But they were unusually silent, saving their energies, glancing now and then at the door to the back room. The younger folk looked much as you would expect teenagers at a disco to look. But older men and women, who came shuffling awkwardly in, had the glazed expressions of folk in a hypnotic trance

At last Hamish McReay opened the door, and the three musicians took their places on the low platform. At the other end of the room, trestle tables were loaded with food.

Robert gave the lead, and the trio went into a slip-jig of Irish origins. Then a lilting strathspey. A young couple danced lightly, laughing. One elderly woman began quietly clapping in time.

It was going to be all right, after all. A chore, to be dealt with and dismissed. A dull little local hop, nothing more. Get it over with, have a good night's sleep, and tomorrow morning start out early for Hexham.

As they played on, the tempo quickened. Robert found he was playing in dance rhythms that he had never come across before. His fingers kept escaping from his control, indulging themselves in fiendish double-stopping and wild swoops down a scale that had never existed before. Over and over again in the middle of a whirling passage the bow would strike the same two harsh, mocking notes of the deadly augmented fourth — the forbidden tritone interval, which in medieval times had been condemned as the creation of the Devil. Some spirit was working within his head and within his fingers, stabbing out weird harmonics, double-stopping, and savage *col legno* bouncing off the back of the bow across the strings. And Deirdre's cascades of accompanying chords became a whirlpool lashing all of them into a fury. The mellow tones of Fiona's flute were becoming an eldritch shriek.

The dancers swung more wildly and laughed more loudly. The older people, still seated, began stamping their feet, stamping faster and faster to urge the players on.

Suddenly the clarsach, almost drowned

in the racket, gave up. Deirdre sat doubled up, shaking her head, refusing to go on.

Robert and Fiona flung aggressive arpeggios and devilish trills at each other, like jazz musicians in a cutting session, until a roar and clatter of applause brought them to a brief halt.

'He's back again,' said an elderly man at the back of the room, 'just the way he said he'd be. Coming back to life.'

Robert started playing again, but after two exuberant reels he found himself alone. Fiona had stopped playing, to run out onto the floor and into the arms of one of the dancers, one of those boys as dark as a gypsy. They had made a dizzying three turns of the floor when Deirdre roused herself and ran out to pull them apart. Clinging to Fiona, she looked up at her husband.

'Robert, you must stop now.'

Robert was aware of a mutter of discontent, but he finished a phrase with a sustained trill and then, putting his fiddle down and demonstrating to the audience how his damp fingers needed drying out, he began wiping them on a handkerchief as he marched off towards the bar.

Several men were offering him drink. With sweat dripping from his forehead, he desperately needed a couple of pints, yet even before he was halfway through the first one he felt the world floating around him in strange swathes of sound — sound that he could somehow see rather than hear. And behind it laughter, triumphant laughter: not reassuring laughter, but something foul and derisive.

Voices muttered close to him, some flattering, some suspicious. 'Better than that feeble laddie we had to make do wi' last year. Would ye not be agreeing that's the true voice, truer this time? Will he be cheatin' on us . . . ?'

A middle-aged man to Robert's left said: 'Ye'll be another who'll nae come back?'

'Well, we do have a pretty full programme, this year and next.'

'But if ye dinna come back, there'll be something missing from that programme. Something . . . or somebody. He has no patience with those who won't keep him alive.' The man leaned closer, in the manner of so many public-bar soaks determined to confide a cherished belief at length. 'Just before his death, Calum of the Clachan said that he'd do no more moving on. But somebody must come each year to keep the tradition alive. Let them come, and he'd be here to guide their fingers. He'd be ready to wake and take part again.'

Robert was engulfed in an overpowering weariness. Somebody — Deirdre and Fiona, or Hamish McReay? — must have carried him upstairs. He knew nothing further until the morning, when he turned over with a groan to find the space beside him empty. Gingerly he eased himself out of bed and peered out of the little window.

Deirdre was just lifting her clarsach into the back of the Volvo. She went round to slide into the driver's seat, and he heard the familiar purr of the car starting, without any trouble. Then she was driving slowly down towards the church.

Deirdre took the clarsach carefully out of the car and carried it into the church and along towards the resting place of Calum of the Clachan. For a moment she fell faint. The sagging woodwork and pallid colours had been rejuvenated. The wood shone as if newly polished. The bands of red and green were bright as if someone overnight had vigorously repainted them.

Still, she had to do what she had come to do. She settled herself on the end of a pew, bent over her clarsach, and began a keening, crooning lullaby from the far reaches of the Hebrides. The gentleness of the harp became slowly louder, the strings fighting against her fingers, while a draught whistling round the church interior became a mocking laugh. She fought down the fear, and went on singing and playing until an indignant voice attacked her from behind.

'Isn't it enough that you defile the ears of my flock with your abominations of yestereve? Now you bring those blasphemies into my church? You're playing that infernal thing a lullaby!'

'I was attempting an exorcism.'

The minister's bitter laugh was as derisive as that other whistling laughter. The echoes of Calum of the Clachan refused to die, but would go on dancing, skittering in and out of the columns, through the dusty old organ pipes, vibrating in the windows. And the minister was staring hopelessly at the colours on the tomb. Would they fade over the coming year, until someone was forced to play the music of madness and bring them back to life?

'You've never thought,' Deirdre said, 'of . . . well, opening up the coffin? Just to see whether . . . ' She faltered, unsure of what she was daring to suggest and what he, in the depths of his soul, was trying to believe or disbelieve.

'I'll not be the one to disturb it.' That was all he had to say.

Now all Deirdre wanted to do was escape. Out into the open air, staggering under the weight of the harp, putting it back in the car, driving back to where

Robert and Fiona were waiting for her.

'What on earth have you been doing?' Robert demanded.

'I was told to get out.'

'By the minister? He wouldn't be best pleased by having heathen music played in his church.'

'No not him. It was ... *something* ... in the building itself. In that tomb. I was told to get out,' she repeated. 'I was *driven* out, and yet,' she faltered, 'one of us is wanted back.'

As they were about to leave, Hamish McReay came out, persistently smiling. 'I told you the car would start in the morning.' And he took Robert's cheque from his pocket, tore it into shreds, and tossed them into the morning breeze. 'Until next year, then.'

'There's no way we're coming back here,' Robert assured him.

But his voice was as shaky as his hands. He looked down at them and wondered how he could have played so vigorously last night, and how he would ever be able to play again. They were somehow no longer his hands. They were drained of all

126

colour save for a pattern of blue veins bulging up through the pale skin. He was drained, utterly drained.

Deidre said: 'Robert, please. Let me drive. You don't look up to it.'

He had no strength to argue.

As they drove away from Kirkshiel, Robert was silent for a long time, watching the road ahead just as closely as if he were driving. This must be the right road, yet it felt as if they were in an utterly alien land, not knowing what was waiting for them round the next corner.

The first time he spoke was to suggest that they stop for a breather on the edge of a tiny weed-choked lochan. Deirdre took a bottle of spring water out of the cooler bag and some plastic cups out of the glove compartment. It was a routine they had gone through so many times before. Yet it was still alien, each movement an effort.

Behind them, Fiona had taken her flute out. She started playing something that caused Robert to spill some of his drink on to his right knee.

'Stop that! What on earth is it?'

'I don't know. It just came to me, the way it did the other day. Was given to me,' she added suddenly.

Deidre, very calm and self-controlled, said: 'Fiona, do put it out of your mind.'

'I'm not sure that I can.'

At last they crossed the Cheviot Hills and headed for Hexham Parking in front of their hotel. Deirdre looked up at the glowing façade of the abbey.

'We made it.' Robert spoke as if they had been pursued by wild Highlanders and then Border reivers all the way. 'Thank God we're away from that dreadful place.' He was trying to wrench himself back to normality, even to make a wry joke of it: 'At any rate that's one engagement we won't be playing again.'

'True, they're not really expecting you back there, Daddy. But one of us has to go back next year.'

He turned to look into Fiona's eyes, which somehow he could no longer recognize. Through their ivory opaqueness shone an eager, intense challenge.

'You're not suggesting — '

'I shall go back next year. I have to.'

'That's crazy. There's no way I'd let you.'

'It's no good, Daddy. Someone has to keep the music pulsating in his heart.'

'This is obscene. You've let that place get on your nerves.'

His wife touched his arm. 'Robert, I don't think you'll be able to stop her.'

'One of us has to go back,' intoned Fiona. 'And it has to be me.'

'Over my dead body.'

Deidre smiled a smile of infinite love and yet of infinite tenderness, a fateful knowledge coming like grey mist out of the western waters.

'Dearest Robert, I'm afraid that's how it may well be.'

THE BITE OF THE TAWSE

They still went regularly to call on old Dominie in spite of all the pain he had once inflicted on them. Martin McLellan could not understand how grown men who had suffered such sadistic treatment throughout their schooldays could still talk about the old man with such reminiscent affection, and go so eagerly to visit him.

But then, Martin was a bit younger than most of his acquaintances, and had spent his schooldays in England. It was beyond him that they could take pride in relating how savagely they had been bruised and slashed by the tawse, and how they could compare gleeful notes on the Dominie's technique in twisting the edge of the leather so that it bit into the wrist and drew blood.

'And it was nae the boys he disliked most who got strapped worst,' explained Tãm Cameron nostalgically. 'It was usually his favourites.' It was odd, the way he licked his lips — odd, because he had otherwise a dry, coldly pedantic manner as befitted his profession as local procurator fiscal depute.

'He was glad to retire when he did,' added Alistair Blake. 'Just about the time they banned the tawse altogether. It would never have suited him.'

'But how could anyone be educated if that sort of thing went on all the time? How could it help you to learn anything if you were always waiting for a meaningless attack?'

'Ye dinnae understand.'

That was true enough. Uneasily he could only suppose that every sadist needed a regular supply of willing masochists. Yet these were his friends, or at any rate friendly acquaintances, who were slowly welcoming him into a community where his wife was at home and he was being given time to settle in.

They had been drinking and talking in The Carrick Arms. He was the first to get up and leave. Kirstie would have the meal almost ready, and he didn't believe in any macho showing off by keeping her waiting.

The others smiled and waved amiably as he left the bar. He was still unsure how deep those smiles went — whether they were smiling with him, or at him.

It was Kirstie's longing to come back to the town after her mother died that had made him give up his job as junior member of a medical practice in Cumbria. There had been little difficulty in finding a new position here, north of the Border. His father-in-law, now a widower who was glad to have his daughter back close at hand, was senior partner in the clinic beside the Community Hospital and was keen to replace a colleague who had moved to the Western Isles.

After six months or so, it became clear that further steps were expected if Martin was to become thoroughly integrated with the place and its key people.

'You'll have to aim at being elected to the Schiltron Society,' said Dr. Cunningham one evening.

His daughter nodded.

Martin had heard the name mentioned

more than once, in an offhanded way as if he was being sounded out as to how much he knew, rather in the way that Masons drop hints and semi-invitations.

'Some sort of social club for people with time on their hands?' he ventured.

His father-in-law stiffened. 'It has a finer purpose than that.'

'And you'll get nowhere in this town unless you're a member of it,' said Kirstie in a half-joking yet encouraging tone. 'Or so I've always been given to understand.'

One Tuesday morning the secretary of the tennis club came to consult Martin about a mildly sprained ankle. After an appointment had been fixed for physio-therapy in the neighbouring hospital, he leaned back in his chair and studied Martin across the desk as if he were the doctor and Martin the patient in need of advice.

'Some of us are going to see the Dominie tomorrow evening. Care to come along?'

'I don't know him. He'd hardly be interested in me butting in on one of your visits.'

'He's quite keen to meet you. He's been told a lot about you.'

'I didn't know there was a lot to tell.'

'I think it would be a good thing if you made his acquaintance.'

There was some heavy implication behind it. Martin tried to stall. 'I don't know if Kirstie has anything fixed for tomorrow evening.'

'I'm sure she'll understand.'

It seemed inevitable: He would politely go through the motions, and that would be that.

Dominie Jardine's house was set back from a side road out of the town, shaded on three sides by a cordon of larches. When he answered the door, Martin's first impression was of an Old Testament prophet with a long beard, which might once have been white but now was the shade of a tobacco stain. He hunched himself forward like a man with severe spinal trouble, stooping so far that his beak of a nose looked ready to stab down on the hand he was shaking in greeting. Whatever medical attention might have helped to catch his arthritic problems in time, Martin had no recollection of seeing any record of visitors to the clinic.

The four men who had accompanied him waited like awestruck pupils until old Jardine nodded that they might sit down. He ensconced himself in a leather armchair with a small table beside it. There was no glass or ashtray or book or anything on the table other than a thonged leather tawse. Martin stared at it in a moment's disbelief, then looked away.

'Ye'll be settling well into our community, Martin?' Jardine's voice crackled like the wind through dry leaves. His eyes were as yellow as old parchment as he stared at the newcomer.

'Finding my feet, yes.'

'Your feet, hey? We usually begin with the hands, don't we, Sandy?'

The landord of The Carrick Arms nodded eagerly, his breath quickening. 'Aye, sir, we do.'

'Then let's begin, shall we?'

The Dominie reached for the tawse, shook it two or three times if to remove any dust that might have accumulated since it was last used, and waited for Tam to hold his palm out. The crack of leather against flesh was accompanied by a gasp from the others — a gasp of appreciation rather than fear. Sandy stared straight ahead, biting his lip and then allowing himself a proud glance at the red mark deepening across his palm. Jardine's grip tightened, and this time the tawse struck sideways across Tam's wrist, and struck again, and again, until blood began to ooze slowly out.

'Ah,' Jardine whispered. He stooped forward, his head coming slowly down until his lips dipped into the trickle of blood. He sipped, and sat back. Then he turned suddenly on the secretary of the tennis club. 'And what are ye smirking at?'

'Nothing, sir.'

'Nothing? And what's there to smirk at in nothing? Hold your hand out. Nay, laddie, the left one. We indulged the right one last time, didn't we? Mustn't show any favouritism.'

The tawse struck again. And again. This time the blood came more readily and showed more brightly against the man's pale skin.

Dominie Jardine's head dipped again in ritual obeisance.

The other two men waited. Martin, incredulous, watched as Tam Cameron held his hand out without waiting to be ordered.

Jardine shook his head. 'No good being greedy, little Tăm. I'll deal with you when I'm good and ready.' Jardine kept him waiting, stroking the strap slowly and lovingly. 'Now,' he said at last, 'let's see how well you remember your homework. Tell me . . . who was the first Stewart king of Scotland?'

'James the First, sir.'

'How many times do I have to tell you? It was Robert the Second.'

'Sir.'

The hand was offered; the tawse rose and fell, rose and fell. The blood trickled out. Jardine's head was lowered. Tam Cameron's eyes closed, and he seemed to be singing to himself.

'You're lucky I didn't lay this across your bare arse, you scunner.' Suddenly

Jardine turned towards Martin McLellan. His yellow eyes had somehow gained strength and intensity. There was nothing misty or weary in his gaze any more. 'What about you, laddie? You'll be joining this sorry bunch?'

Martin had difficulty in finding words. 'I don't think so.'

There was a whimper of reproof from the other four.

'Ye'd be considering, maybe, that you're not ready?'

'I don't think this is a very healthy pursuit.' Martin tried to assert himself. 'Speaking as a medical man, I couldn't condone — '

'Ah.' Dominie Jardine was echoing him mockingly. 'Speaking as a medical man? Well, when you've thought it over, do come and pay me another visit. And until then, ye'd best be keeping a still tongue in your heid.'

Whether that stillness was meant to include his wife, Martin did not know; but in any case it was unthinkable that he should not tell her what had happened. She listened in silence, her hazel eyes perplexed and beginning to look apprehensive.

'It was downright obscene,' he concluded. 'Sick. That depraved old man has a very unhealthy hold over those perverts.'

'No worse than the Masons,' said Kirstie. 'Baring your chest and rolling up your trouser leg and taking bloodcurdling oaths. What's so different?'

When he spoke to his father-in-law and senior partner, the response was much the same. And Dr. Cunningham reminded him of that earlier warning. 'You'll get nowhere in this town unless you join the Schiltron Society.'

'But what's that got to do with Jardine's sadistic practices? And what the hell does 'Schiltron' mean?'

'The practices you call sadistic are simply initiation rites which are repeated at regular intervals to keep the pulse of the society still beating. And the schiltron, as every schoolboy ought to know, was the formation of spearmen designed by Robert the Bruce, standing close together and forming a hedgehog with their spears sticking out from each side to draw blood from anyone foolish enough to attack. Purely symbolic today, of course.'

Martin found himself studying his patients for symptoms other than the ones they related to him. How many of the men complaining of prostate trouble or of irritated bowels were members of that society? Members of the Rotary made no secret of their membership. He already knew the names of the board of the local football club, the tennis club, and the Chamber of Trade. But he did not know how many of them had been educated — in several distinctive ways — by Dominie Jardine. Once or twice he was sure the local grocer was grinning at him; and behind his back he sensed heads turning, shrugs, sly smiles.

Wondering how long it would be before he cracked?

Out of the blue one evening, Kirstie said reproachfully: 'I'm regarded as a freak, you know.'

'Who by? Who on earth . . . ?'

'The women in the sugar-craft club, and the charity coordination group.

They're friendly enough, but I can tell they're wondering why my husband hasn't joined the men who count. They're obviously wondering whether you weren't considered good enough to be invited.'

'There was an invitation, but I turned it down.'

'Do you want people to go on sneering at me?'

He endured another fortnight of her bewilderment and her sadly submissive yielding to his lovemaking, then said reluctantly to Tam Cameron that he was wondering whether he might go along with them to another meeting with the Dominie.

Jardine's bleary eyes offered a welcome so moist that he might almost have been in tears. But his voice was clear and gloating. 'Of course, being a new boy, you'll have to have a very harsh lesson to bring you into line. After the basic rite, the renewals are less stringent.' He stroked the tawse. 'Perhaps you'll be good enough to take your shirt off.'

So Kirstie was right. Not all that different from the Masons, after all.

Until, as he draped his shirt over the back of his chair, the four who had accompanied him launched themselves on him from behind and forced him head down over the back of a low couch. They held him firmly as the tawse lashed across his bare flesh. He clamped his teeth together, swearing that he would not cry out. Would not even wince. But after he had lost count of the strokes that were lacerating his skin, he opened his mouth and screamed.

The others began laughing. And, as if the scream had been a signal, four mouths began dabbing greedily into the blood that he could vaguely feel oozing from him in sticky patches.

He must have fainted for a few seconds. When he recovered, the four men were affectionately lifting him back into an upright position, and Tam Cameron was gently slipping his shirt back over his aching, blistered shoulders.

Dominie Jardine was on his feet, too. There was a faint red smear on his lips, and his eyes were brighter and younger than ever before. 'Your turn for a booster,

Alistair. A booster — that's what they call it in medical terms, isn't it, doctor?'

Alistair Blake held out his hand with a flourish matched by Jardine's flourish of the tawse. He stood immobile, not flinching, until the skillful sideways swipe of the leather drew blood from his wrist. Then the Dominie beckoned Martin forward.

Blake was holding his hand towards him, palm upwards; and Martin, in a haze, found himself stooping and tasting the salty blood. For a moment he was so dizzy that he felt he was likely to collapse. But when he straightened up, they were all smiling at him in a new comradeship.

'Welcome, Martin,' said the Dominie. 'Good of you to join us. And you must join us at our monthly dinner next Wednesday, too. And you must bring your wife. I'm sure she will feel at home with our other lady guests.'

That night Kirstie cried over the weals across his back, but kissed them, and then urged him into making love with more ferocity than he had ever known.

At the dinner on Wednesday, in a large

private room at the hotel, there were so many faces he knew, and so many things he knew about each of them. Thomson with his gout, Maxwell with his early testicular cancer, and a good half dozen of them with high blood pressure. Some he would not have expected to be members of anything other than a minor tradesmen's social club. And their womenfolk — full members, or just wives here on sufferance?

Dominie Jardine presided over the proceedings with a benevolent smile. His eyes were bright and clear. Who had had the honour of providing him with a booster before his arrival at this evening function?

Placed between two of the women, Martin talked inconsequently to one about her son's ingrowing toenail, and listened to the other on the subject of flower arranging. Every now and then he smiled at his wife, sitting opposite, and received a radiant smile in return. She was obviously unworried by the attention he was paying to other women. She was happy. Happy and confident.

The babble of conversation was cut off so suddenly that one would have thought a switch had been snapped over. Dominie Jardine had risen to his feet and was staring at Martin. He made a wide sweep with his right arm as if inviting Martin into his embrace.

'Perhaps our new member will come and stand beside me.'

There was a smattering of applause as Martin awkwardly extricated himself from his chair and edged along the table to take his place beside the Dominie.

'And his good lady.'

Kirstie rose and moved towards the two men, her lips parted, gliding almost like a dancer. Martin saw her through a strange haze. Everything was in slow motion. He tried to get a grip on the everyday reality of his surroundings and all these ordinary townspeople. What were they expecting of him and his wife? Were the two of them supposed to go out on to the small square of polished floor and the honour of being the first to dance?

Kirstie's shimmering silver dress was lower cut than he had realized when they set out this evening. Her breasts and throat were a dazzling white, infinitely brighter than he had remembered.

She reached him, and smiled, and put her head back to offer her throat.

He could bear the beauty of it no longer. Such exquisite whiteness had to be marked with the triumphal redness of life.

His mouth moved towards her waiting throat, still but for a rhythmic pulse of anticipation. His lips drew back from his teeth. He entered her as a lover, and felt the warm spurt of her blood. And heard a sigh of deep sensual pleasure running around the room.

When at last he withdrew and she looked adoringly into his eyes, her father was standing beside her, much as he had stood on the day she married Martin.

'This is a wonderful day,' said Dr. Cunningham. 'A day of fulfilment. I always felt it had to be her husband who would finally consummate their marriage in this way. It had to be carried out with a husband's love, not merely as a father's duty.'

Everybody was laughing and congratulating the happy pair, and Dominie Jardine was edging forward, diffident yet purposeful, to ask if an old man might kiss the bride. The kiss was aimed at her throat.

As the company broke up into chattering little groups, Martin and Kirstie stood holding hands in the middle of one group, until there was another sudden silence. This time it was Dr. Cunningham who had something to say.

'I am in the position to make a truly rewarding announcement. For some years our community has been neglected because of some very odd bureaucratic interference. Somebody, somewhere, was raising doubts about the — ah — quality of what we had been providing in the past. But I am happy to tell you that next month the Blood Transfusion Service will be resuming its visits to us, asking for volunteer donors.'

There was a surging chorus of delight.

Dominie Jardine declaimed above them: 'It is time to offer our blood and knowledge throughout the veins of others. This

will be the greatest of all charities.'

In the heart of the jubilation, Kirstie pressed herself impatiently against Martin. 'Let's go home. It's been a wonderful evening. Let's make it an even more wonderful night.'

THE PROVOKER

They met in a park, discreet and casual as before, sprawling on the grass above the lake. Krastev asked for a light. Jackson nodded abstractedly, held out his lighter, and went on watching the children, with their toy boats and their jam-jars full of weed and cloudy water.

Krastev lay back and said, 'You have thought it over?'

'Yes. A lot of thinking, believe you me.'

'And you are ready to start?'

'I'm sorry. I can't do it. Can't possibly.'

In this profession you could never really be sure that anything was going to work out the way you had planned it; yet Krastev had allowed himself to grow fairly confident about this one. Jackson had seemed ripe for the plucking. Now, obviously, there was further work to be done.

He inhaled, let the smoke drift from his lips, and watched the wind snatch the fine plume away.

'There are drawbacks we have not discussed?' he ventured.

'The whole thing. It's just not on.'

'Please tell me.' More coaxing, more gentle prodding, the preparing of new temptations and sweeter reassurances. 'I am sure that neither of us wishes to close the door.'

'Look,' said Jackson, 'if I did work for you, it'd be because . . . well, we've gone all over that. You know I'm fond of your country. That's how it all started. But I wouldn't be in your country. I'd still be here — and asking for trouble.'

Yes, they had indeed gone over all that. Krastev thought it had been settled. But if it had to be said over and over again, he would say it.

'We can come to an arrangement. That has always been in our mind. You do two more years at the Centre, that will be enough. Perhaps only one year. It will depend,' he murmured, 'on how much you bring out for us. We would not wish to endanger you for too long, in any case. Then if you wanted to . . . to . . . '

'Defect?'

156

'Emigrate, shall we say? If you wished to emigrate, there would be a comfortable home and a job for you. Nothing too demanding. Somewhere near the Black Sea, one of the places you so much admired. That would be the least we could offer, yes?'

Jackson sighed. It was, Krastev knew, more than three years since he had been away. His job in the Centre ruled out those idyllic trips. The Security boys had been critical enough at the start over those visas stamped in his passport. He had been put through a whole series of gruelling interviews before acceptance. With his scrawled signature acknowledging his obeisance to the Official Secrets Act, he was barred from going off gaily on any holiday trips to Eastern Europe, however innocuous they might be.

'Can't be done,' said Jackson.

Krastev quelled his rising irritation. He could not afford to lose Jackson now. He took pride in his manipulative skill. Jackson was still within his grasp, and there must be a way of tightening that hold.

He, too, sighed. 'I am disappointed. You did not mean the things you told me.'

'I meant them all. But this deal — no, it's just not on.'

'You are frightened you would be discovered?'

'It's a hell of a risk, you've got to admit.'

'Two weeks ago you told me how you hated to think of your country taking the lead in the development of these terrible plague organisms. You wished that there should be no such weapons of war, or that if they were to exist then everyone must have equal access. Like the atom bomb, the hydrogen bomb. All or none.'

'I still feel that way.'

'Then why . . . ?'

He truly longed to have a complete explanation, so that all the loose ends might be tied up in his mind. Not just because the failure of this job would impede his own career, but also because of this intense personal commitment to Jackson. He liked to feel that, if any question about Jackson were fired at him, he would be able to answer without having to think twice, and, even more, that if Jackson himself had a question there would be a soothing way of answering, of steering him gently at last, to the place where he ought to be.

'It's not just me, you know,' said Jackson now. 'There's Marjorie.'

Yes. Inevitably there was Marjorie. So many times, in jobs like these, a woman's name cropped up. Sometimes a hindrance, sometimes a help. Marjorie was a hindrance. He had known it from the start, but had hoped that Jackson could be coaxed round or over this stumbling-block.

Carefully he said, 'You think your wife could not be happy in our country?'

'She wouldn't have a clue.'

'Please? You think she plays the detective — a clue?'

'It's just a phrase.'

Krastev would have liked to pursue this. He delighted in the acquisition of new idioms. Austerely he refused to be distracted. He said, 'She was with you on your holidays?'

'Once. Another time her mother was ill,

and she insisted I took a couple of weeks on my own. She was marvellous about it.'

'Admirable.'

'Then there was the time I went to that conference on pesticides. I stayed on for a week. That was when I really got the feel of the place.'

'You could teach her to love our way of life, just as you do.'

'It'd be an awful shock for her,' said Jackson. 'Honestly, it wouldn't be fair. She hates moving. We agreed this move would be the last. She's settled here. Really settled. I'm sure I've told you how crazy she is about the house — the painting we've done, the garden, all her gadgets — she's just beginning to get things right. I really couldn't uproot her.'

'And you? You are satisfied?'

'Well, I don't know. Who *is*? Look, if I could break away, know there was an end to it . . . But it's not so bad really. It's a comfortable sort of routine, a sort of . . . well, you know how it is?'

Krastev knew. He had dropped each item of information into its appropriate slot over these last few months, and could have recited unprompted the whole calendar of Jackson's days and nights, his weeks and months. Every day the walk of less than half a mile to the gates of the Centre; the ritual production of his pass, even though every guard knew him by sight; the work, the tea break, the canteen lunch, the coffee in the afternoon; the Tuesday morning conference and the obligatory round of drinks each Friday evening between six and six forty-five. A night shift two nights a month, and one weekend in three when he must stay at home as duty supervisor within reach of the telephone.

Then there was the chess club meeting on alternate Thursdays, the annual cricket week with the local electrical fittings factory, the occasional Saturday or Sunday fishing up the river. Once or twice, a weekend in London at a special meeting, or at a hush-hush symposium in the Midlands.

A man in a shabby blue suit, incongruous in the bright, if cool, sunshine, sauntered along the path beside the lake. Krastev wondered, as he had wondered before, whether Jackson was ever followed. He doubted it. His own sensitive antennae would have warned him. They couldn't follow everybody, every moment of their spare time, in and out of shops, homes, cafés, pubs and parks.

Jackson got up, brushing flecks of grass from his jacket. 'Well, that's about it.'

'We will arrange another meeting soon.'

'There really wouldn't be any point.'

'But I enjoy your company. It is a pity if we cannot be friends.'

Jackson flickered an uncertain half-smile at him. 'I must say I've enjoyed it, too.'

'I am glad. So glad.'

He liked to believe that their elusive, incongruous friendship had a special significance, far beyond that of Jackson's relationship with his wife. Krastev surely understood Jackson better than that unimaginative woman could ever hope to do . . .

In the train on the way back to London he conjured up a picture of Marjorie, based on a couple of snapshots Jackson had shown him, which would give him something substantial to dislike. It was clear from all Jackson said and didn't say that marriage, for him, had become no more than a set of stock responses. His emotions had flowed into a conventional mould and set there. He had married the woman, presumably because he had loved her, and then they had sagged into ordinariness, stifled any rebellious desires and dissatisfactions, and adjusted with polite resignation to each other's boredom.

Krastev stared out of the window, rubbing the knuckles of his right hand to and fro above his right ear. It was one of Jackson's mannerisms. He liked copying Jackson. Sometimes copied him without knowing it, which kept him naggingly on the subject of Marjorie.

Marjorie, who was so impossible in shops; Marjorie, who collided with people on pavements because she never looked where she was going; blindly erratic Marjorie who was too irresponsible to be allowed behind the wheel of the car; who left junk on the stairs, fiddled obsessively with household chores without regard for their relative importance . . . oh, he knew Marjorie. Jackson had told him all about her — told him sporadically, with an offhand laugh which was meant to be ruefully affectionate and quite failed to make it sound funny.

Jackson was valuable. Too valuable to be lost because of a self-absorbed, banally domesticated woman. For the sake of a whole defence programme he had to be coaxed onto the right path. And for his own sake, thought Krastev with genuine affection.

★   ★   ★

Luchezar said, 'Still you maintain there is a chance of recruiting him?'

It was as though he were hoping Krastev would admit defeat, so that a black mark could duly be recorded against him.

'I know him by now,' said Krastev. 'I am sure that basically he wishes to join us. He is romantic about our country and our system, and unhappy about his own.

He is an idealist.'

'An idealist. Like ourselves, of course.'

'Of course.'

'Yet he will not take this crucial step.'

'Not as things are at the moment.'

'There is no way of applying pressure?'

'He is not the kind of man who would be useful to us under duress. If we employed threats, he would at once cease to co-operate. Not,' added Krastev wryly, 'that there is anything with which to threaten him. It is simply that, as long as his wife lives . . . '

'Ah,' said Luchezar.

He sat back and contemplated his Deputy Commercial Attaché, which was how Krastev was accredited to the Embassy. Luchezar had eyes as dark as a gypsy's, but it was a cold darkness. Trapped in that stare, you longed to retract whatever you had said and confess your error and swear to do better next time, even when there had been no error. Krastev tried to return the gaze steadily and to keep his voice steady, too, when he said, 'Yes, I think the wife must be removed.'

'You are telling me that the wife must be killed,' said Luchezar. 'We try to avoid that kind of thing. One slip and there is trouble for all of us. At home they would not be pleased — not at all pleased.'

'Then there must be no slip. If we want Jackson, it is the only way.'

'We do want Jackson.'

It was as near as Luchezar would get to issuing an order, or even to concurring. From now on the full responsibility was Krastev's.

He felt the tingle of fear and exhilaration he had felt a few times before: the swift attack in Ankara that sweltering summer four years ago, the quiet savagery in Tehran, and the incident in Belgrade that almost went terrifyingly wrong and then worked out so splendidly. His whole body seemed to throb. When he left Luchezar he was drunk for a few minutes. Then his mind cleared and he sat down to evolve the foolproof means of getting rid of Marjorie.

Once she was disposed of, he was sure Jackson would prove amenable. There would be no personal loyalty — a reluctant loyalty at best — to confuse his thinking.

The important thing, the absolutely essential thing, was that neither the police nor Jackson should suspect there had been a calculated murder.

Above all, Jackson. He would be appalled. As a matter of principle — a great man for principles, Jackson — he would probably break off all relations with Krastev. It had to look like an accident. And afterwards there must be continued caution. He could not rush up to Jackson, saying brightly that that was that and when could Jackson start work, please? There must be discreet sympathy, and equally discreet intimations that Jackson's friend was still his friend, not forcing the issue but always there in case he was needed.

Oh, the sweet subtleties of violence! Krastev had to admit that he was in his element. He derived a rich, sensual pleasure from this awareness. Every master craftsman likes to be employed to the full stretch of his powers. The task ahead was one of delicate, complex carpentry, and all the more worthwhile because of those complexities.

An accident. Krastev mused, shaping one set of possibilities after another, and discarding one after another.

A hit-and-run driver? Too clumsy, the aftermath too unpredictable, the dangers too uncontrollable. A fire in the house? But how to ensure Marjorie was at home, Jackson out, and the escape routes blocked? To truss her up would be too risky: the fire might be put out too quickly; the charred remains of such bonds might be identifiable.

A fall? From where, to where? And how to guarantee it would be fatal? A car smash? But Jackson didn't let her drive. And again, it was difficult to guarantee fatality. Serious injuries were no good. Death was essential.

Was he *quite* sure Jackson would succumb, once Marjorie was dead? No possibility that Jackson might be deeply shocked, might drudge on with his work numb and deprived of all ambition, might lose all the energy needed to make the break?

Krastev banished the thought. He was sure, quite sure, that Jackson regarded Marjorie as a dead weight round his neck. After the initial regret, which any decent man would feel, he would learn to breathe again . . . and to think clearly.

An accidental shooting? But so few people in this country carried guns that a shooting of any kind required a lot of explanation. Everything, thought Krastev with a rare nostalgia for his homeland, was so much easier in the Balkans.

★　★　★

That evening he decided to concentrate on the question of opportunity. Let the necessities of the timetable dictate the method.

Anything attempted while Jackson was at work, and Marjorie at home or shopping, would probably need to be in daylight, with any number of potential witnesses. If the blow was to be struck while Jackson was on nightshift, the date of the nightshift must first be established

— and without arousing his suspicions.

His chess club night? Krastev viewed it soberly from every angle. Possible, but risky. A meeting might be cancelled or might finish early. Jackson might arrive late or leave before the end. If he got home too soon, or even dawdled and went for a stroll, which human beings have an infuriating habit of doing, he might throw out all the calculations and even be suspected himself. That would never do.

If the timing was too tight, there could all too easily be an echo of that case of the Liverpool insurance agent (who, recalled Krastev with the pleasure one derives from noting a dramatic coincidence, had also been a chess devotee) or that man in Suffolk. Both of them, one in a city and one in a village, were nearly convicted because of questions of time and the inexplicability of their movements.

Krastev was a connoisseur of English murders. Beneath their smug surface, the English seethed with inventive perversity — the most ruthless killers, emotional exploiters and cheats. He could not understand why Jackson should wish to leave such a stimulating country. But the deal, once securely made, would be honoured.

Just as he was trying to work out a way of checking on Jackson's movements over the next few weeks, the Embassy received a letter from a John Black asking for details of cultural package tours.

Perhaps there would be no need to kill Marjorie after all.

John Black was Jackson. Krastev had instructed him to use this procedure if ever he wished to get in touch. They would answer discreetly, without danger.

Early that evening Krastev left the Embassy and made his way to a distant public callbox. He rang Mr. Black about this Irish holiday inquiry, asking for further details. Mr. Black said it now happened that he had to come to London the day after tomorrow, so perhaps he could call in — if he hadn't left it too late to make a booking.

'You have not left it too late, Mr. Black.'

'I can probably get there about eleven. Will that be all right?'

'We shall look forward to helping you then, Mr. Black. Goodbye.'

He must have changed his mind; must have decided to work with them, Marjorie or no Marjorie. Krastev could hardly wait to find out. He reached Regent Street ten minutes early on the morning of their appointment and strolled slowly up and down, looking in windows at the blurred reflection of the Aer Lingus offices on the other side of the road. There was a brief traffic jam. Two tall buses obscured his view. When it cleared, he saw Jackson apparently coming out of the main door and pausing, like a man who has settled his business and now is in no hurry. Then he strolled slowly away. Krastev kept pace on the far side of the road. He was sure there was nobody following Jackson.

They met at last in Vigo Street, nodded with mild surprise and sauntered on like old acquaintances with a few minutes to spare.

Krastev said, 'We were glad to hear from you.'

'I thought I ought to come clean with you,' said Jackson, 'rather than wait for you to find out.'

'Find out?' It had an ominous ring.

'I've decided to quit the job.'

Krastev smiled. 'A year from now, perhaps. After you have — '

'You don't get it. I mean to get right out. I'm sick of it. I don't want any part of all this biological murder any more.'

'But that is what we agreed.' Someone jostled between them, separating them. Krastev trotted to catch up. 'You stay on — such a short time it will be — and then you are free, you live where you want, we make everything easy for you.'

'Sorry,' said Jackson. 'I'm getting clean out.'

'Please. You must think this over.'

'My boss says that, too.'

'You have told them? Already?'

'He wants me to go away for a weekend and work it all out.'

Away for a weekend. Krastev had a flash of hope. Silently he thanked the enlightened enemy who had ordained this, and aloud he said, 'On that, at least, we agree. You must not make sudden decisions. Harmful decisions.'

'Trouble is,' laughed Jackson, 'he's coming with me. Oh, he swears he won't try to sway me at all. Not much! We'll go fishing on a friend's place in North Wales, and he won't try to influence me — except with salmon and whisky and hock and reproachful looks.'

'This weekend,' said Krastev tentatively.

'Next weekend, actually.'

'And your wife . . . ?'

'She's scared stiff. I've told her I want to pack in the job. She hopes old Manson'll talk me out of it.'

'You told me it was because of *her* that you could not possibly move,' Krastev accused him.

'I can get a job at the Agricultural College. Ten miles each day, but I've got the car. The money isn't as good, so Marjorie's not too happy. But at least we can stay in the same house.'

They turned down Bond Street, walking slowly side by side towards Piccadilly.

'It's your doing, Krassie,' said Jackson unexpectedly. 'It's really you. You've helped me to see how deadly the whole set-up is.'

Krastev went hot and cold as he thought what Department SRB would say if they heard this. Hoarsely he said, 'I want nothing that is not good for you.'

Jaokson looked at the traffic, at passers-by, and flickered a strange, sheepish look at Krastev. 'I really believe you mean that, Krassie. But you do understand?'

'I thought I understood. I understood you wished to come in the end to live in my country.'

'I've told you. I couldn't ask Marjorie. There's just no way. Unless . . . '

'Unless?'

'No, nothing. Things like that don't happen.'

Krastev went even colder. Had Jackson guessed — was he actually daring him to go ahead? It was unthinkable. But the jolt, the mere fleeting idea of it, made Krastev extra wary. From now on he must choose every word carefully, listening to

Jackson's plans and making sure he triggered off no sensitive alarms.

' . . . safe to leave her for a whole weekend,' Jackson was saying in that unconvincingly bantering tone which Krastev had learned to recognize. 'I don't suppose I'll get much coherent thinking done. Too busy wondering if she's managed to burn the place down.' He waved at a plate glass window as though to prove a point. 'She'd go mad over that gimmick in there. Mad about any electrical gadget. You should see our kitchen: whizzers and whiskers, mixers and moppers, floor-wetters and floor-polishers . . . you name it, we've got it. I tell you, she'll blow herself up one day. Always connecting and disconnecting. She's a push-over for any sharp salesman. Do-it-yourself? Do-for-yourself, more likely.

He was chattering breathlessly as though to block any further discussion of the real subject.

Krastev, steering them back on course, said earnestly, 'Do not make up your mind until you have come back from your weekend.'

Ought he to have said that? Would Jackson remember it after, link it with other remarks, ask what it had meant and start to wonder?

'Between you and me,' said Jackson, 'I can't believe any of old Manson's arguments are likely to sway me.'

'Or any of mine?'

Jackson began to walk faster. 'If I had my time over again,' he said. 'If . . . ' But he could not finish.

When they shook hands, Krastev's eyes were moist. In a moment of strange intensity it seemed to him that Jackson wanted to say something, wanted somehow to apologize: to expiate the guilt of having let him down.

It was all right. Krastev's spirits rose as he walked away. He would reclaim Jackson. It was all going to work out just as he had planned it.

* * *

His luck was in. The Saturday of the crucial weekend brought a steady drizzle. Women did their weekend shopping in the morning, and stayed indoors in the afternoon. There was only an occasional car swishing down the street, the pavements were almost deserted, and it was reasonable for a man to walk with his hat pulled down and his raincoat turned up.

Krastev padded up to each front door and pushed a leaflet through each letterbox. If any bored woman, twitching her front window curtains, was ever asked to give evidence about that afternoon, her recollection of a stranger delivering leaflets about a well-known washing powder would have no relevance. Every few houses, Krastev took out a clipboard and scribbled on the paper attached to it. He might just have come from talking to a selected housewife; or he might not.

At last he reached the house whose number he had long known by heart. He pressed the doorbell. He was sure that Marjorie had chosen the triple chime that resulted.

He opened his case and took out the board again; holding it against his coat to protect it from the rain, hunching so that he looked as dejected as any man on this degrading sort of job had the right to be.

Footsteps shuffled along the hall. The door opened.

Marjorie was flabbier than the snapshots had led him to believe. Lines tugged downwards from her eyes, and her mouth managed to be both thin and slack. Her glasses had blue frames, tipped with two spiky flourishes of mother of pearl.

'I am sorry to disturb you on such a depressing afternoon — ' His smile sought her condolence, and failed. — 'I am carrying out market research on electrical appliances.'

'In this weather?' She leaned on the door so that it could be quickly closed. 'You're foreign,' she said with a pout of distaste.

'Our organization specializes in the distribution of contemporary fitments from the Continent.'

Marjorie said, 'There was a programme on television, not a week ago, saying there were all sorts of people coming to the door with tall stories.'

He nodded. 'I quite appreciate your

caution, madam. All I want is to ask a few questions.' He inched his way in under the mockery of a porch, and poised his ballpoint pen. 'Now — do you have a washing machine?'

'Of course,' said Marjorie indignantly.

'Twin tub?'

'Yes.'

He made a tick in one of the columns. 'An electric mixer?' When she proudly nodded, he asked what make it was and nodded approvingly himself, and then went down a long list. Marjorie's brusque answers mellowed. He smiled his admiration, and now she was ready to smile back.

Abruptly she said, 'Look, the ink'll be running on that form. And how can you write with gloves on?'

'Oh, I can make sense of it later.'

'Why don't you come inside, just for a minute?'

'Really, I . . . ' He shrugged self-deprecatingly. 'Just for minute. It is most kind of you.' As the door closed behind them he glanced down and said, 'Oh, you still have those . . . ' He cut the sentence short, and made a note on the paper.

'Those what?' A fat, two-way adapter stuck out of an equally bulky socket in the skirting board, carrying two plugs. One was not in use, the other trailed a length of flex towards an ornamental lantern on the hall table. 'They take up so much space,' said Krastev.

'Well, I need the adapter for when I use the vacuum cleaner. And when it's cold we keep a convector out here.'

'Of course. But with the new slimmer fitments . . . '

'I don't think I've seen any.'

Krastev put the clipboard on the table and opened his case. He took out a three-way adapter and tilted it in his palm so that she could see how slight it was. Marjorie said,

'So it's all an advertising stunt after all.'

'By no means, madam. Our market survey is being carried out on purely scientific lines. But I will be frank with you: it is connected with the introduction of our new range of fitments.'

Krastev rolled the words over his tongue. It gave him a guilty thrill to be able to indulge himself so flagrantly in the most heinous kind of capitalist jargon, like an austere atheist surrendering drunkenly to the splendours of St. Peter's. He had practised his role assiduously and almost believed himself as he went on, 'We wish to estimate the resources of the average household and the number of fitments generally run off existing power points. The average house-wife . . . ' He smiled, and was delighted by her immediate reaction to his diffi-dence. She waited for the compliment, and he delivered it. 'Not that you are the average housewife, of course, I can see.'

She was eager for a demonstration of the new adapter.

'If you have two or three items of kitchen equipment,' said Krastev, 'per-haps a refrigerator, a cooker?'

She led him down the hall and into a gleaming kitchen. He glanced quickly at the long window above the sink. Trees sheltered it from the adjoining fence and the house beyond.

Marjorie indicated an adapter with plugs sticking out from the wall at shoulder level. There was another one jutting from the skirting board, feeding the refrigerator and a toaster standing on a plastic-covered work surface. Krastev ignored her gesture, and chose the second. He bent and pulled the adapter out.

'Do take your gloves off,' she said. 'It's warm enough in here.'

He gave no sign of having heard her, but laid the new slim-line adapter on the floor, with two equally compact plugs beside it. Then he patted his pockets. 'I would demonstrate, but I have no screwdriver. I was not really intending to make this a sales visit.'

Marjorie pulled open a drawer. She took out a screwdriver and, as though for luck, a pair of pliers. 'I don't know why we're going through all this. I mean, honestly, I'm not going to buy anything. I don't know why you're bothering.' But she watched him, and then, as the screwdriver slipped through his gloved fingers, she said impatiently, 'Oh, here — let me do it.'

He let her retrieve the screwdriver. She loosened the retaining screw from the plug of the toaster and freed the wire. With a brief, appreciative examination of the new plug, she connected the wires to its terminals.

Gauging his moment, Krastev said, 'It's best to see the adapter in the socket before inserting the plug. That is what I particularly wished you to test. The clip action is quite new.'

She looked up as though to argue this, then inserted the adapter. She bent over it, the plug in her right hand. Krastev moved casually closer to the wall. Marjorie pushed the stubby pins of the plug into the adapter. They stuck. 'I thought you said they clipped in?' she said, instantly derisive. 'Why, they're stiffer than . . . ' She got a good grip, and pushed.

Krastev stabbed out with one rubber-shod foot and flicked the switch down.

Marjorie appeared to pivot on the plug. An invisible rope wrenched her into an agonized loop. She drew her lips back and her eyes glared — not at Krastev, not at anyone or anything. Her glasses fell and crunched beneath her elbow, then her hand was jerked free and she was hurled to one side, her neck bent, her eyes still open.

There was a faint wisp of smoke, an acrid smell. Krastev flicked the switch off. A scorch mark blackened the floor and a few inches of woodwork. He took out the adapter and plug, disconnected the wiring, and dropped the samples back into his case. He reconnected two leads to the original plug, ensuring that the earth lead went to the wrong pin, and frayed the insulation of the third. With a gloved fingertip he rubbed some of the blackness further along the skirting board, and studied it for a moment. He would have preferred something more immediately impressive. He opened the cupboard beneath the sink and found a plastic bucket. He filled it from the tap and left it on the draining board while he moved Marjorie's body into a more appropriate position . . . When he left the house, he turned in the doorway as though talking to someone, put his hat on, raised it politely tugged the door shut and walked slowly to the gate. He made time to scribble industriously on his clipboard, then methodically put leaflets in all the remaining letterboxes on this side of the street. What he had left behind in that house was a bit confused. No natural death is other than confused. The neat murder, with no rough edges, is the suspect one.

At the inquest, Jackson's sorrowful recollections of his wife's ineptitude with electrical gadgets confirmed the rest of the evidence. The late Marjorie Jackson had clearly been tinkering with a plug, had wired it wrongly and somehow started a small fire from a short circuit, and then fatally tried to put it out with a bucket of water, electrocuting herself and scorching an area round the power point. It was pure chance that there had not been a major blaze.

The coroner, returning his verdict of death by misadventure, issued a warning to unskilled members of the public not to dabble with technical matters best left to skilled craftsmen. He also expressed his deep sympathy for the bereaved husband.

★　★　★

Krastev waited a fortnight before venturing to express his own sympathy.

From a callbox he telephoned Jackson at home. 'I was most upset when I read the news about Mrs. Jackson.' He did not give his name. There was no need.

Jackson said, 'Oh. Oh, yes. Nice of you to ring.' Then cryptically, 'I thought I'd be hearing from you.'

They met, discreet and casual as before, above the lake in the park. Krastev was taut, but happy. There was all the tension of a lovers' tryst on ground fraught with past associations.

'This must have made a great difference to you,' said Krastev.

Jackson watched the boats and the jam-jars, and said: 'Naturally. Bound to.'

He sounded so calm. Krastev hesitated, then plunged. 'This may not be the right time to discuss it — I would not wish you to make hasty decisions — but you do know that our offer still stands? You know we are prepared to help in any way, every way?'

Jackson chuckled. 'You're a right old opportunist, aren't you, Krassie?'

'I have told you, we do not wish to rush you into decisions now, but we would like you to be confident — '

'Oh, that's all right,' said Jackson. 'I've made my decision.'

Krastev's heart pounded. 'Yes?'

'I told you a few weeks ago. I'm getting out.'

'You are not still thinking of that 'Agricultural College'? Not after . . . after what has happened?'

'Much further away. Get the whole grubby mess off my boots. Sell up the house, start all over again.'

'But this is ridiculous! You cannot do this. You joke with me. To walk out like that, when we have got so far, you and I — no, that it not possible.'

'Let's not get emotional,' said Jackson. 'I know we did toss ideas to and fro, and I was keen — truly I was — for a while. But . . . well, I'm sorry, but — ' He used the idiom which had once amused Krastev and now enraged him. ' — it's just not on.'

'I do not understand.'

Jackson was abstractedly watching a

woman walking gracefully and unhurriedly up the slope. 'Don't suppose you ever will. Perhaps we all make the same mistakes over and over again.' His condescension made Krastev feel far more murderous than he had felt towards poor, superfluous Marjorie. 'But somehow I don't think so.'

The woman reached them. Jackson got to his feet and kissed her. She was not a great deal younger than Marjorie, but was buoyant where Marjorie had been flaccid, quiveringly alive as Marjorie could never have been.

'Christine, I've told you about Krassie, haven't I?'

Krastev lurched to his feet, silently swearing that it must not be true. 'You cannot mean what I think! You told me, so many times you told me, if you had your time over again — no, you cannot be throwing all your ideas away because of . . . ' Words failed him; breath failed him.

'We all reshuffle our priorities from time to time,' said Jackson. He was waiting to shake hands, coolly preparing to say goodbye. Krastev stepped back. He could not bear to touch that outstretched hand.

'If you knew how much I have done for you!'

'I'll think of you,' said Jackson, 'often. You know, I suppose we owe you our little holiday — a few weeks in Ireland before we get reorganized. That last time we met I rather fell for some of those brochures that they had in that office.'

'If you knew. If I were to tell you . . . '

Jackson's smile was tinged with the sheepishness he had half revealed before. Suddenly, warmly, he said, 'I'm glad we had chance to meet again. I've been wanting to thank you. We're both so grateful.'

'Both?' It was no more than a whisper. 'Grateful?'

'I never thought you'd do it. Honestly, I never really thought you'd do it.'

Jackson tucked Christine's arm through his. They walked away. At the foot of the slope they turned around and waved to him.

★　★　★

In the Embassy, Luchezar said, 'It did not occur to you that he was meeting another woman?'

'There was no indication. I do not see when — '

'His chess club evenings, for a start.' Luchezar spoke like a disillusioned teacher exposing the failings of a supposedly advanced pupil. 'Did you ever verify that he went to chess? And what about those weekends?'

'There was never a hint of anyone else.'

'Evidently it was not only his wife he was deceiving.'

'I trusted him. I knew him.'

'You were wrong to trust him,' said Luchezar, 'and it is plain that you did not even begin to know him.'

'He won't get away with it. We must show him.'

'To what end? He cannot be forced to work for us. And to dispose of him as an example . . . as an example to whom?'

'You do not mean we leave it at that? Nothing happens at all?'

'All that happens,' said Luchezar, 'is that you prepare to return home on tomorrow's flight.'

'But there is no need. In everything I have been very careful. There is no suspicion whatsoever — I am not *persona non grata*.'

'Not with the British,' said Luchezar silkily.

At the door, Krastev was tempted to make a dash for it. Out to the nearest police station, to ask for asylum, to confess to murder. Better an English prison than what might be waiting for him at home.

But he would never get past the Embassy gates. And he had covered his traces so well that he could produce no evidence to support a confession of murder. He had done his job too well. Only one thing had gone wrong.

He thought of the traitor Jackson, and wanted to weep. Behind him, as he opened the door, he heard Luchezar's voice as though from a great, melancholy distance.

'I wish we had succeeded. I admire your Mr. Jackson very much. We could do with men of that calibre. Such a pity.'

POOR CORA

'But you won't tell her, will you?' said the young man. 'You won't tell Cora?'

Miss Gertrude Blane opened her eyes. There was an unpleasant taste in her mouth, and her back was hurting. She had been asleep but would not for the world have admitted it — certainly not to a stranger. She blinked across the compartment. The train rattled through a small station, and shadows flickered across the face of the young man who sat opposite.

What had he been saying to her?

'Of course I won't,' she said hurriedly.

'We don't want her to know, you see.'

'No.' Her old voice was thin and harsh after the cheerful sound of his youthful voice. She wished she could remember what he had been talking about.

'I knew you'd understand,' he said with a smile of relief.

She couldn't even remember how she

had got into conversation with a total stranger.

But was he a total stranger? His face was not unlike that of someone she had once known. Harry? No, Harry hadn't been seen for ages ... Harry, she abruptly realized, had been dead twenty years. She was glad *They* hadn't heard her thinking about Harry: *They* were always accusing her of losing her memory, and of course her memory was as good as it had always been.

Surreptitiously she unfolded the crumpled slip of paper that was tucked inside her glove and read the name of the station. She said casually:

'How long is it before we come to Brayhurst?'

'You have another little snooze,' he said. 'I won't leave you behind. Don't worry.'

His insolence made her wriggle irritably in her corner. She didn't even know him, yet here he was talking as though he was looking after her.

She said: 'Young man — '

'My name's Peter, Aunt Gertrude,' he

said in the tone of one who had reminded her of this fact several times already.

She was silent. He knew her name. He was certainly not her nephew, but he spoke as though he were one of the family. She blinked out of the window, seeing the scattered outposts of a town, a huddle of villas around two or three stumpy church towers. *They* were concerned in this: *They* knew something about it. Perhaps this young man had been deputed to look after her.

She drew herself up.

'Here we are,' he said. 'This is Brayhurst — got here sooner than I expected.'

He took her small case down from the rack — had he perhaps put it *up* there for her in the first place? — and said: 'You haven't left anything, have you?'

She did not reply. Now she thought about it, carefully picking up her thoughts and studying them, holding them as it were close to her eyes and squinting at them, she realized that he wouldn't have mentioned her niece Cora if he hadn't been one of the family.

There was something she must tell Cora.

No, that was wrong: there was something that Cora mustn't be told. She wished she hadn't fallen asleep.

'Here's the car,' said Peter. 'In we go.'

She wished he would not address her as though she were a small child in need of encouragement. Moving more slowly than was necessary, merely in order to impress him with her self-sufficiency, she got into the car that was waiting outside the station.

'Off we go,' he said.

I am going to see Cora, she thought, sitting upright on the edge of the seat although it brought on the pains in her back. She must take stock — collect all the items of knowledge concerned with this trip — build up an explanation of what she was doing here today.

Brayhurst. Cora lives at Brayhurst. But she can't, she's married now. Yes, that's it, Cora and her husband are staying with my brother Richard — Cora's father — and this is some sort of special occasion. Of course, perhaps Cora's husband . . .

The words popped out before she could restrain them:

'You're Cora's husband.'

'That's right. My name's Peter.'

'Of course your name's Peter,' she snapped. 'I know that perfectly well.'

The car turned out of the main shopping street and went up a hill towards a cluster of woods, from which protruded large houses set in their own grounds, hiding from one another in the shelter of haughty trees. She recognized Richard's house as they came to the top of the hill, and thought how annoyed *They* would be to know that she really and truly remembered it right away.

Her brother came out to meet her. She was shocked by the lines on his face. He walked as boyishly as ever, but he was old — and yet, she thought, Richard was younger than herself. *They* must look at her, at Gertrude Blane, and think that she too was old.

Gertrude shivered.

'Come along inside,' said Richard. 'You're looking well, Gertie. It was nice of you to insist on coming.'

Yes, she had had to insist. Bobbing up and down in the corner of her mind, now clear, now faint, was a memory of that argument. 'But Gertrude,' *They* had said, 'you've missed Richard's last five birthdays — why worry about this one?' And she had tried to explain that she and her brother had always spent his birthdays together, ever since his dear wife died. 'But you don't,' *They* had said — 'You haven't seen Richard for ages, so be a dear and forget about it. Richard,' *They* had unforgivably said, 'won't want to be bothered on his birthday.'

And then, she remembered, she had cried, and *They* had said 'Oh God, she's off again,' and someone had spoken to someone else on the telephone, and at last it was agreed that she should come down for her brother's birthday.

She was so glad it was all clear now.

Except for that thing that she must not tell Cora.

She said: 'How is Cora?'

'She's very well. It's nice to have this double celebration — Cora's first wedding anniversary and my sixtieth birthday.

Sixty eh?' He grinned. He was genuinely pleased to see her. She loved her brother. 'Let's see — you haven't seen Cora and Peter since they were married and had that couple of days in town, have you? Grand lad, Peter.'

A girl wearing a linen frock and a loose green cardigan came in. She had her father's ready smile. Gertrude recognized her at once and said, delighted: 'Cora, my dear — '

'Don't say you've forgotten your favourite?' Richard laughed. 'This is Marion, the one you used to spoil.'

'Dear Marion. My, how you've grown.'

They kissed one another. Marion had grown up. And Cora — coming in behind, walking with Peter, holding out both hands and saying, 'Aunt Gertrude, it seems ages,' — Cora had grown up. The two girls were strangers now: she did not know them as she had once known them. She wondered why this thing had happened to her, and automatically turned to Cora's husband, the young man who had been sent to fetch her.

'You're a lucky young man,' she said

conventionally, though that wasn't what she really meant at all.

Just by looking at him she could see that he wasn't good enough for Cora. She distrusted him: he was too cheerful, too free.

Not that she had ever really liked Cora, who had been the noisy one of the two: Marion had been her favourite, talking to her, and listening to her. Cora wouldn't listen to anybody. Cora was the one who had been overheard, saying: 'Aunt Gertrude — dotty, you know . . . '

She turned suddenly and saw Marion and Peter winking at one another. Cora was not looking. Cora did not see her husband winking at her sister.

Peter said, 'Ah, Aunt Gertrude.' And he nodded knowingly.

What was it that she must not say to Cora?

She stared suspiciously at Marion and then at Peter. This wasn't the same Marion. She didn't like that wink, that glance of complicity. There was something between the two. Something that Cora mustn't know . . .

'How was Uncle Stephen when you left?' asked Cora. 'And the others — all well?'

'Oh, yes,' she said bitterly, 'They are all right. They never have anything wrong with them.'

All they do, she wanted to add, is sit around and wait for me to die, hoping I'll leave all my money to them. Why should she? Here were the only people she was really fond of. Dear Richard. Dear Marion. Poor Cora.

Yes, there had been something in that glance that Peter and his sister-in-law had exchanged that made Cora seem pitiable. On her first wedding anniversary, too.

Treachery, thought Gertrude. She had known right away that it was this Peter who was responsible for the changed atmosphere of the house. Marion and Cora weren't little girls any longer: they weren't the two girls who had been here when their Aunt Gertrude had visited so often; and it was the stranger, the invader, who was responsible. He had no business here. He did not belong.

'And so,' said Richard across the table,

'tomorrow is our great day. It's a good idea to make one's daughter get married on one's birthday — '

'I'm not so sure,' protested Cora. 'Now we only have one party instead of two.'

Cora had always loved parties. She wanted fun. A shallow child — and she hadn't even the eyes to see what was going on in front of her, on the eve of her first anniversary. Poor child.

Why, why had that shameless young man taken Cora's aunt into his confidence? Why let me into his dreadful little secret? thought Gertrude.

Cora was passing a plate. She had never been fond of the girl, but now it was impossible not to feel sympathy for her. It was easy to understand Peter — naturally he would prefer Marion, who was the finer of the two, but he ought to know that it was too late now; he had made his choice, and this sort of conduct was inexcusable.

'They've grown up, Gertie,' Richard challenged her. 'My little girls have shot up, haven't they?'

'And yet they're still so alike — in

looks. When I think of them standing together, in that little picture you used to have of them — '

'Don't, Aunt Gertrude,' said Cora. 'Don't lump us together. Marion's Marion, and I'm me. We're not at all alike.'

Of course, of course. She had forgotten how touchy little Cora had been, how determined not to be classed with her younger sister. And now that same younger sister . . .

Gertrude tried to intercept other glances passing between the guilty pair, but they were now averting their eyes from one another and looking cleverly unconcerned.

They had the impertinence to look to her for approval. She was in their secret — or, rather, she would have been in their secret if she hadn't fallen asleep in the train while Peter was talking. Why, why?

Her thoughts were running away with her. Unless she sat very still and quiet, she would be lost in that lamentable confusion again, and *They* would laugh and say 'Oh God, she's off again'. So she sat still. If there was an answer to all this, it would come when she was quiet and receptive. She waited, sitting with her head cocked, quizzical as a parrot.

Peter, married to Cora, was in love with Marion. Marion, who had once been her favourite, encouraged him — that smile and wink! Ah . . . that was it!

He knew that Marion was her favourite and that she disliked Cora: Cora might even have said that her Aunt Gertrude hated her, because Cora had always been a fussy, exaggerating sort of child. Peter wanted to get rid of Cora and marry Marion. Perhaps — Aunt Gertrude's face wrinkled into its network of dark lines, etched deeply with horror — perhaps he was not worrying whether he married her or not, so long as he got the money . . . Because, of course, they had all guessed that most of Aunt Gertrude's money was going to her favourite, Marion.

Poor Marion. Poor Cora. Both of them bewitched by this plausible young ruffian. And Richard, too.

Gertrude wondered what she was going

to do. The young scoundrel had thought she would approve because she was so fond of Marion, but he must be shown that his mad idea was wrong. Something must be done quickly, before her memory blurred again: an hour hence, she might not be so sure of everything; it would all have to be thought out afresh.

She kept herself tensely calm, not talking too much and not giving way to any excitement.

But there was nothing she could do that evening. Possessed by the fear that in the morning she would remember nothing, or would have to rack her brains for hours, she made a note on a piece of paper of the essential facts, and glanced at them first thing on awakening. They were clearer and more irrefutable than ever. There was no possibility of doubt.

She got up early and let herself out of the house for a walk in the garden, thankful that *they* were not here to watch her, to fuss insincerely about her rheumatism and the dampness of the morning and this and that and the other.

It was Richard's birthday. She had

brought his present, a beautiful briar pipe, downstairs with her and left it on the table so that he would see it at once, just as she had done when she was a little girl and it had been Christmas or birthday time.

No present for Cora. She was sorry about that, but then, she hadn't known about Cora's wedding anniversary. People ought to tell her. Still, she might be a great help to Cora in another way.

'Aunt Gertrude, surely you oughtn't to be out as early as this?'

Here, incredibly, was that young man. What was his name? Peter, of course . . . and the name resounded in her head. This is the young man who invites your approval of his love for his sister-in-law, believing that you care so much for her and so little for poor Cora that . . . But she must not get excited, or it would all fly away.

'Afraid I'll catch a cold and die?' she chuckled.

'Now, then.' He took her arm and led her towards the goldfish pond. 'I don't think you ought to be wandering about.

Come on, let's take a turn round the pond and then go in. You know what today is. And mind you keep our secret' — he squeezed her arm — 'because you know what Cora is. I saw a film once in which . . . '

His voice went on and on. They turned around the end of the pond, and as they came up the other side she could control herself no longer. She broke into the flow of his words. She said:

'Secret, indeed! Not tell Cora . . . why, you — '

And because she couldn't think of anything sufficiently bad to say, she pushed him. He hadn't expected anything of the sort. He had treated her as an accomplice, regarding her as a wicked, indulgent old woman — how could he have been such an arrogant fool? — and now he was falling towards the water, his head down, his arms out. His feet twisted under him. He groped for something that wasn't there. His head struck the sharp stones on the edge, and he lay still. The water clouded with a red, creeping cloud, fuzzy at the edges.

Gertrude was suddenly calm. She was not at all sure what had happened, but she knew that somehow everything was all right. She sniffed appreciatively, inhaling the sweet morning air as she walked towards the house and in through the open French windows.

'There you are, Gertie.'

'Aunt Gertrude, look!'

Cora was prancing before her, as she had always done. Such an exhibitionistic child, thought Getrude. But the coat was undeniably beautiful.

'Such a perfect fit,' said Cora. 'So right. I'd never have believed that Peter could get something so exactly right.'

Richard came over and thanked his sister for the pipe.

'And where's Peter?' demanded Marion.

'Where — ah, where?' Gertrude knew. Or did she? Already the memory was fading. She frowned, wondering about Peter, that unpleasant young man: she knew something about Peter that the others didn't know, but for the moment she couldn't recall what it was. Only that it was a good thing and that a weight had been lifted from her mind.

Marion was beside her, speaking quietly. 'It does fit so well, doesn't it?' she murmured. 'Peter said he'd told you all about it in the train. He's almost as excited about it as Cora is. But you know what Cora's like — if she knew I'd helped Peter to choose it, and tried it on, she'd have been furious. She's certain that we're not the least bit alike, and she's always accusing me of being too fat, so — well . . . But it's just right for her, isn't it? And I was so careful about the colour. Men never really understand these things, do they? It does you good to see Cora so pleased. I wonder where Peter is? It's time he came to receive his applause, however unmerited.'

Gertrude twisted her hands nervously together. Yes, it was time Peter put in an appearance. She was sure she had seen him somewhere. He ought to be here.

Not that he was good enough for Cora: not even for silly little Cora.

Gertrude began to feel uneasy. She remembered that she had seen Peter in the garden, and she wondered if she ought to go and fetch him. But she did not make any move. Somewhere in the back of her mind was the idea that she knew something about Peter — something the others wouldn't like.

MISS MOUSE AND MRS. MOUSE

The quarrel had begun at the party and continued in the car on the way home. At the party it had been a silent conflict — after you've been married for six years you can have a flaming row without making a sound and without letting anyone else see what's going on; but in the car it got noisy.

It was not about anything in particular. After those six bristling years it didn't need to be. Lucille had proved to be a shrew. She was jealous, she was petulant, she was easily offended. Arthur had given her no cause for jealousy but this did not deter her. Indeed, perhaps it accounted for her petulance. When you have no good grounds for a row, you get irritable at the effort of having to concoct them. And her readiness to take offence was possibly due to Arthur's patience with her in the early years; patience could be interpreted as condescension, which in itself was an affront, even an insult.

Anyway, with Lucille there was no need to look for trouble. She had plentiful reserves on which to draw.

Her voice resounded against the back wall of the garage. It echoed through the hall as they went toward the elevator.

It was long past midnight. Arthur said, 'Do keep your voice down.'

'Frightened of the neighbours now?'

'Not frightened. Just that *I* wouldn't want to be awakened by a drunken woman yelling at this time — '

'I'm not drunk. You're the one who's drunk. Maudlin. Soggy with it. And half asleep — '

'If I am,' said Arthur, 'I must be the only one.'

They went up to the fifth floor. Their front door opened into a narrow hall that broadened into an L-shaped sitting room. Immediately inside was the door to their bedroom. As Arthur opened it, Lucille began again.

'Anyway, that's the last time I go to a party with you. The last time.'

'Suits me.'

'Shoving yourself away in a corner and talking to men all evening. You're a bore. You heard me, a bore! Talking to men the whole time.'

'You seemed to be talking to men the whole time, too,' he observed.

'That's what parties are for. Just because you're undersexed — '

Arthur said, 'Shut up, will you?' He jerked his thumb toward the closed door of the small bedroom beyond. 'You want Miss Mouse to hear?'

'I don't care who hears!'

'Then it's time you did care. It's time you learned to behave like a civilized human being.'

'I'm not good enough for you, am I? Not up to your lofty intellectual level. Not — '

'Shut up!'

'What'll you do if I don't?'

She was beyond reason. She was almost dancing up and down, wanting no logical outcome, no victory in argument, wanting only the physical sensation of anger and the rasp of her own voice in her harsh throat.

'Shut up,' he said, 'or one day I'll — '

Because he could not finish the threat, he opened the door into the smaller room. Even demented as she was, surely she could not carry the battle into their little boy's bedroom? It was not just a matter of waking Danny but also of transmitting their shameful antagonism down the microphone to their baby-sitter at the other end of the building.

Lucille sighed histrionically. She was enjoying the frustration as much as the release.

Arthur bent over the crib in the darkness and turned Danny over on his side. It looked as though things had been quiet tonight. Danny had not tried to climb over the side of the crib and go exploring. Unless, perhaps, he had made such an attempt and the distant Miss Mouse had had to come running to tuck him back in again.

Cautiously Arthur lifted the microphone and trailed the wire into their own bedroom. Lucille waited, glaring. He closed the door softly and put the microphone on the dressing table. Only then did he speak. They never 'signed off' in Danny's room. He was a light sleeper, and the murmur of a familiar voice close to him almost invariably jolted him into wakefulness.

'We're back, Miss Cobb.'

There was a faint click as the baby-sitter pressed the reply button, and a quiet, rather drowsy voice said, 'Haven't had any trouble. He hasn't stirred. Good night.'

'Good night,' said Arthur, 'and thank you.'

Lucille waited, allowing a decent time to elapse after these formalities and giving the baby-sitter time to switch off the loudspeaker at the other end of the wire. Then she returned to the attack.

Arthur gave her two minutes before interrupting. He did not attempt to answer her accusations. He hardly heard them. Lucille's impassioned onslaughts had become as routine as taped music, playing background tunes so familiar that one no longer consciously followed the notes; they were just there. Somewhat over-amplified, but dulled by the resistance built up over recent years.

Arthur said, 'It would be fun if Miss Mouse hadn't switched off at her end, wouldn't it?'

They called her Miss Mouse so consistently between themselves that he sometimes feared they might address the girl by that name to her face. The name fitted her so well. She lived with her aged mother in the cramped couple of rooms described as a bachelor apartment at the end of this large building. From their windows on the fifth floor Arthur and Lucille could look down on London's forest of new skyscrapers and old spires and power station chimneys between the trees on the hill. From their windows four floors down, on the corner, Mrs. and Miss Cobb had a view of the garage roofs, one patch of the communal garden, and a high wall cutting them off from the next building,

At the moment there was a long sagging loop of wire curving down from the window here to that window some sixty or seventy feet away. There might even be another wire crossing it or coming in from a different angle. Miss Cobb supplemented her income by listening in to the cries or silences of children in different apartments of the building when their parents wanted to go out. She was timid and quiet, but reliable. Tomorrow morning she would come shyly round with the loudspeaker, help to roll in the wire, collect her fees, and scuttle away again; and doubtless there would be somebody else needing her services tomorrow evening. Sometimes she had as many as three separate loudspeakers in her apartment, and assured the parents that even if all three babies cried at once she would be able to cope.

'She'd be too scared to eavesdrop,' said Lucille. 'Might do her good to try. Though she wouldn't learn much about the gay life from you. Or about anything else.'

Arthur was tired. He wanted to go through the usual ritual of washing, cleaning his teeth, getting into his pajamas, and going to bed, letting her words wash over him until she gave up in disgust. But something urged him toward disaster.

'Hadn't realized what a nice voice she has,' he said.

Lucille dropped her earrings with a clatter on the glass top of the dressing table.

'Oh. Started to fancy Miss Mouse now, have you?'

'I simply said she has a nice voice.'

'You'd make a good pair. You're the mousey type yourself.'

He said, 'Do you suppose she and her mother sit up waiting for us to get back? Or d'you suppose she's in bed?'

'Imagining her in bed, are you?'

'Now that you mention it — '

'I saw you with that girl at the party tonight. Pitiful. And now Miss Mouse.'

'Ten minutes ago you were saying I spent all my time talking to men.'

This remark, being logical, was ignored by Lucille. You never won a battle of this kind by being logical.

'If you think you're going to have me tonight,' she raged, 'and pretend all the time it's that blonde — or Miss

Mouse — God, but you're a twisted little creep!'

He had never thought of Miss Mouse in any such way. But now, since Lucille was virtually goading him into thinking of her, he conjured up a picture of the girl. Still a girl, though she was easily near thirty. He often saw her crossing the concrete in front of the garages with her rather schoolmistressy walk, her school blazer looking pathetic on someone her age, her straight yet not unstylish brown hair, her almost masculine briskness. But when she pushed the door of the garage up and over, having to reach up for the final thrust so that her calves were tight and strained, she did not look masculine at all.

He said, 'Can't say I've ever fancied her. But let's be fair — she hasn't got a bad figure. She'd probably have made someone a good wife if it hadn't been for that suffocating old mother of hers.'

'Peeping,' breathed Lucille. 'Snooping. Drooling over her. You make me sick!'

He was sorry he had ever allowed this to get started.

'You're talking rubbish,' he said wearily, 'and you know it.'

She was pulling her slip over her head. It muffled her voice but didn't stop her talking. 'You're a pervert,' she mumbled, 'that's what you are — a dirty little, warped little — '

It went on and on. The slip got stuck, and as she wrestled with it her denunciations grew more and more obscene.

He could stand it no longer. Suddenly he hit her.

It was almost comic. His blow caught her in the ribs and winded her. She stumbled about the room gasping for breath, sobbing impotently as she tried to free her arms, incapable of standing still and calmly extricating herself.

She swore again and ran blindly at Arthur. He held her off. She tried to scratch him, but the movements of her arms were too restricted.

She threw herself bodily in his direction. Arthur put both hands on her waist, twisted her, and threw her back.

Off balance, Lucille shrieked and went down, her arms pinioned in an unnatural position. Her head struck the edge of the dressing table. There was one incredibly sharp crack, then a duller thud as she hit the floor.

At last she had stopped shouting. At last she was still.

Arthur said, 'Lucille?' He stared for a moment, then went on his knees beside her. 'Lucille?'

She was not going to answer. No abuse, no derision, no fury. No questions and no answers, never again.

Arthur pushed himself away, half crouching. The edge of the bed jarred his spine. He hauled himself up and sat on the bed, shaking.

There was a silence such as he had never known. It was not just that Lucille had at last stopped yelling and gone to sleep. There was no breathing, no faint rustle of life, none of the hundred and one shufflings and fidgetings of everyday existence. He had not realized that death took people so far away so swiftly and completely.

He listened, as though to snatch some last whisper back from eternity.

In the next room the crib creaked. Arthur got up and took a step toward the door. Then he waited. Danny had turned over, but there was no further sound.

It was just enough. As though a relay had clicked into place, Arthur found himself turning and hauling Lucille's corpse up from the floor. He tore the slip away from her and pulled her arms down by her side. He straightened her out and pulled sheet and blanket over her, tidying them and making them look as natural as possible. In case someone called? Absurd idea. In case Danny came toddling in?

He felt sick, and went to the bathroom.

After throwing up and washing his mouth out, he went into the sitting room and poured himself half a tumbler of whiskey.

He must not panic. So many times he had read of sudden death making people do stupid things. He was going to sit calmly in his usual armchair and think it out. There were several hours of the night still ahead of him. By morning he would have decided exactly what he must say and do.

Get her out, get the car round and drive her away somewhere, dump her?

That was ridiculous. He had nothing to be ashamed of. It had been an accident.

But would people believe that?

The urge to get the car out and drive madly somewhere, to take immediate action, was almost overwhelming. He couldn't just sit here.

But he couldn't go out and leave Danny alone. Ask Miss Mouse to baby-sit? Wake her up and ask her to listen in again while he went out for a drive? Just want to dispose of a corpse, Miss Mouse. Won't be long. I'll be right back.

Think.

He took a long gulp of the whiskey and tried to concentrate.

Telephone the police? Tell them everything?

Manslaughter. How many years for manslaughter?

Accident, he said to himself over and over again. It was an accident.

Believe me.

And if they didn't?

It wasn't fair. They wouldn't be fair to him. None of them would. Nothing had ever been fair. He had always had a rotten deal, all his life.

Again he drank and again he told himself slowly and firmly that he must concentrate, he must think.

He closed his eyes.

When he opened them again, it was daylight and he could hear Danny whimpering. It was not a cry of distress, but simply his morning moan, a combination of annoyance at being awake and eagerness to see a friendly face.

Arthur got achingly to his feet.

He looked round the sitting room and was incredulous. The ordinariness of it was grotesque. He could not believe Lucille was dead. He went into the bedroom and waited for her to heave resentfully over in bed and groan at him.

She lay still. If he tugged the sheet back, there would be a slight dribble from one corner of her mouth as there always was. And then she would sullenly open her eyes and scowl at him.

He pulled back the sheet.

Her face was impassive. Where her head had struck the edge of the dressing table there was a hideous black bruise, and a caked stream of blood ran down the side of her neck.

Danny began to squeak: 'Dink. Dink.' He was ready to be given his morning bottle of fruit juice.

Usually Lucille prepared this before going to bed. Last night she had not done it. Arthur went out to the kitchen and went through the motions. He carried the bottle in and was greeted by a broad smile. Danny clung to the side of the crib and shook it vigorously.

Arthur found himself going mechanically through the normal Saturday morning routine — partly Lucille's routine, partly his own. He put Danny on his pot and wiped his bottom, dressed him, and carried him out through the master bedroom. The little boy peered curiously over his father's shoulder at the motionless shape in the bed.

'Mummy's sleeping,' said Arthur.

Danny accepted this. His stock of words was still small and his powers of assembling them were insufficient for him ever to come out with coherent, damaging evidence. He was only two; his pleasures and his comprehension were all of the immediate moment, without past or future.

Arthur prepared breakfast for both of them and then got out the toy box and let Danny spill the contents all over the floor.

Decide, decide — he must decide. But although his hands and feet obeyed him and he was carrying out all the normal tasks automatically, his mind was numb.

Danny lumbered across the floor toward their bedroom door. Arthur intercepted him and steered him away. He must keep that door closed. Danny was tall for his age; he could reach up to door handles now and turn them.

Each of the inner doors had a keyhole, but the keys had never been used. Where were they? Arthur explored, and found one in a plastic truck at the bottom of Danny's toy box. It fitted. Arthur locked the bedroom door from the outside and pocketed the key. He had a picture of

Danny going in, running to his mother, prodding her —

He fought it off. It couldn't happen now.

It was early in the morning for a drink and there was still a foul taste in his mouth from last night. But Arthur poured himself a large whiskey and sat in the same chair, trying again to concentrate.

Every thought he attempted to grasp and hold on to became nonsense when he looked round the room. Everything was so ordinary, so usual-looking. There was no place here for anything so melodramatic as a corpse.

It was all so ordinary and usual that he hardly reacted to the sound of a key in the lock of the front door.

It was one of the ev… sounds you took for granted. Bu… ha… he … clicked shut he sudde… bell. Ju… was impossible. This … might … coming back from sho… 'Oh.'

He was on his feet … girlish came into the room. S… appeara… square grey plastic … 'I did speaker. Murdo…

2…

'I thought I'd better return this,' she said, putting it down on the table. 'And this — which I didn't have to use, of course.' She held up her right hand. The front door key dangled from its wire ring on the joint of her little finger.

It was a mild morning but he felt a chill. The normality had begun to warp. Surely Miss Mouse didn't behave like this as a general rule? She was not the type to let herself into someone else's home without knocking or ringing first. Lucille would certainly have discouraged it, and would certainly have mentioned it to him. For Miss Mouse to let herself in if Danny cried into the microphone was one thing; for her to come barging in during the daytime was quite another.

On edge, Arthur heard himself say, 'I'd ave thought you'd — well — rung the ust in case — well, you know, I have been — '

Her laugh ought to have been and diffident, to match her nce. But she was oddly confident. once walk in on someone. The ks. They came home late one night and forgot to tell me on the wire. I heard noises in the speaker and thought it must be the baby, or even someone who might have broken in. So I hurried round and let myself in very quietly and crept through. And there he was — ' Her eyes dilated. 'Naked,' she said.

'Embarrassing.'

'Yes.' But she was still laughing. Her eyes were pale grey. He had never known before that gray could be a fiery, scorching colour.

His head throbbed. He said, 'I hope we didn't keep you up late last night.'

'That's quite all right. I was waiting for the Bentleys as well. They were much later than you.' She glanced at the loudspeaker. 'I must take theirs back, too. I meant to bring it with me when I came.'

Danny looked over his shoulder at her. He had feigned indifference for a minute or two, but now he wriggled backward so that he was close to her right leg. She patted his head, stiffly yet possessively.

'Who's going to look after the poor little mite now?' she asked abruptly.

Arthur's throat closed. The implications of the question could not possibly be what he knew them to be. She couldn't know! He tried to believe that by standing still and saying nothing he could make everything all right.

Miss Mouse contemplated the little gray box of the loudspeaker again.

He forced sounds out. 'Your mother — I hope she's well?'

'I hear so many things,' said Miss Mouse dreamily. 'If I don't switch off right away, I do get such an interesting picture of our neighbours.'

'But you've no business to — '

'Mother's usually in bed, of course. She loves reading detective stories until she goes to sleep. A good murder story is so soothing at night, don't you think?'

'And you,' he said, 'stay awake. And listen.'

'If people are late getting back, I put the speaker on my bedside table and read while I wait. And when they get home it's often much more interesting than a book. Unless, of course' — she frowned a reproach — 'they leave the microphone in the baby's room all the time. That's a bit of a cheat.'

She drifted away from Danny toward the bedroom door. 'My bed,' she mused. 'Did you really try to imagine what I look like in bed? Shall I tell you what I'm like — show you what I'm like? Do you want to know?'

It was true. She had heard everything. She waited for him to speak but he couldn't make a sound. No words would come out until her hand was on the handle of the bedroom door.

'Miss Mou — er — Miss Cobb — '

'It's all right,' she said. 'I know you call me Miss Mouse. But you don't really think of me like that, do you? You played along with your wife all that time because she was so nasty. But you yourself saw deeper than that. You're right. I haven't got a bad figure. Would you like to find out for yourself?'

'If you go back and throw the wire out of your window,' he said wildly, 'I'll haul it in.'

She gently shook the door handle. 'You'll have to unlock this first.'

'If you throw it out at your end, I can deal with it any time.'

Miss Mouse said, 'She's really dead, isn't she?'

'I don't know what you're talking about.'

'You bullied her. I didn't switch the speaker off and I heard every word. You threatened her and beat her up. You fought for several minutes before killing her.'

He was hypnotized by the pouting little movements of her lips. Full and soft, they puffed the words at him almost lovingly.

'It's not true,' he finally managed.

'The police won't like your story at all — not one bit.'

'It's simply not true.'

'In that case I suppose I might say I heard every word and you were horribly provoked. You were patient for as long as any man could be. Then your wife sprang at you, and in trying to keep her off you accidentally threw her back so that she fell and was killed. Accidentally.'

'That's exactly what happened. You know it is.'

'I wonder which story will sound better?' She put her head to one side and studied him. 'Now may I see her, please?'

Mesmerized, he took the key from his pocket and turned it in the lock.

She walked into the bedroom. He glanced back. Danny was once more absorbed with his fleet of model cars.

Arthur went into the bedroom and quietly closed the door behind him.

Miss Mouse was inspecting Lucille's corpse with bland interest.

The microphone still stood on the dressing table, its wire snaking out of the window on its fatal way toward the Cobbs' window.

Miss Mouse said, 'I suppose one ought to feel sorry for her. She really was appalling, wasn't she?'

'It was an accident,' said Arthur.

'That depends.'

'Depends on what? You *know* it was an accident.'

There was a scratching noise on the other side of the door. Arthur heard Danny whimper, 'Dink. Dink.'

'In a minute,' Arthur called. 'Won't be

a minute, old boy.'

'Dink.'

Miss Mouse said once more, 'Who's going to look after the poor little mite now? He hasn't any grandparents. I know that.'

'You know every damn thing, don't you?'

'Yes, Arthur.' His name was like a caress.

'What are you expecting to get out of this?'

'Just you,' she said. Before he could protest, she went on, 'I'll testify that it was an accident. I heard it all. Entirely your wife's fault. Tragic, but in no way your fault. And after you've recovered from the shock and a decent interval has elapsed — '

'Well?' He could manage only a whisper.

'You'll marry me,' said Miss Mouse.

'I — after what's happened, I don't think — I wouldn't be — '

'I want to get away from my mother,' said Miss Mouse, very matter-of-factly. 'I can't go on. Truly I can't. Let her live on her own. When we're married we'll be able to afford to support her separately — send her away somewhere, see she's in good hands. All she wants really is to lie in bed most of the day reading detective stories.'

'Dink,' cried Danny, growing fretful.

'You'll find I'm quite a lively little mouse, Arthur. Not much practical experience, but — ' She smiled reminiscently, her lower lip moist. 'I've heard a lot, Arthur. The Bentleys, for example. And the Murdocks. The Murdocks are awfully inventive. And they like to talk about it. Things that surprised me. I might even be able to surprise you. You won't find me dull, Arthur.'

There was a faint rattling sound at the door.

'It's Danny.' Arthur seized the chance of a respite. 'I'd better go and take care of him.'

He went to the bedroom door. It wouldn't open.

He tugged. It wouldn't budge. He tugged again, then realized that Danny's curiosity had been too much. Arthur had left the key in the door, on the outside, and Danny had turned it.

'Danny,' he called gently.

'Dink,' said Danny on the other side of the door, but not with any great fervor.

'Danny, the key. Clever boy. You turned the key. Turn it back, will you? Please?'

There was the clatter of two toys being slammed cheerfully together.

'Danny!'

'We're not locked in?' For the first time there was the faintest suspicion of a tremor in Miss Mouse's tone. 'He can't have — you *can* make him let us out?'

'Danny,' said Arthur encouragingly. 'Danny, the key. Come and turn the key again. The key!'

Faintly through the door he head Danny say, 'It's a choo-choo.'

Arthur turned and looked into Miss Mouse's incandescent gray eyes. She held out her hand, with the front door key still dangling from her little finger. 'If we could attract attention, I could drop this down.'

'Fine. And when someone comes to let us out, how do we explain you being in this bedroom with me? We let them in and they see Lucille. Or we don't let them in — and it's a bit fishy. And it gets fishier later when they hear about her death, and you just happening to hear it over the wire — and just happening to be locked in the bedroom with me the very next morning.'

'You think they'd try to implicate me?'

'Sure of it,' said Arthur with a sort of gloomy relish.

'We've got to get out. We've got to get out. On our own, somehow.'

'Tell me how.'

He felt taut enough to snap. At the same time he wanted to laugh. To laugh horribly and for a long time. Once he had started it would be difficult to stop.

And then a metallic voice said, 'If you throw the key of the front door onto the grass, I can come up and let you out.'

They stared.

'Provided,' said the crackly little voice from the microphone on the dressing table, 'that it's understood you look after me. At my age' — the whine was like a shrill oscillation along the wire — 'I need someone near me. And little Danny doesn't just need a father and mother. He needs a grandmother, poor little mite.'

'Mother!' Miss Mouse clamped a hand on the microphone as though to throttle it.

'We've still got the Bentleys' speaker here from last night,' said Mrs. Cobb. 'I thought you were taking rather a long time, so I connected it up to this wire. Just in case you were up to any mischief.'

She was a disembodied witch trapped in the small box on the dressing table. It had heard too much, that box, and now it was spewing up what it had learned.

'Mother, you had no right — '

'Such a silly idea,' said the distant Mrs. Cobb. 'You think you'd get away with it? Telling the police a story like that? They can establish the time of death, you know. I've read all about it. And what you heard over the speaker would confirm it. So why such a long delay before notifying the police? They're going to be very suspicious about that. It will look like a put-up job.'

Now Miss Mouse's eyes were smoky

with uncertainty.

Her mother went on, 'I have a much better idea. If you agree — if you'll take me with you, look after me, *promise* to keep me with you — I'll let you out. And we'll get your wife into your car, Arthur. Drive her off, smash up the car. Say she came home with you last night and had a terrible row with you. And drove off. Both Melanie and I heard her go — we heard the whole thing.'

'Melanie?' he echoed stupidly.

'You'll soon get used to calling her Melanie.'

Arthur glanced at Miss Mouse. Melanie Mouse. He would soon get used to it, would he?

'You've been worried stiff,' said Mrs. Mouse — or Mrs. Cobb, or the witch of the wire, or whatever she or it might be called. 'And now you're going out looking for her. And, as Melanie says, after a decent interval — '

No. He wanted to shout it out loud. The nightmare had to stop somewhere. No! But the shout was still silent, still only within him.

'Dink.'

It was Danny again. He had come back to the outside of the bedroom door and was whimpering.

'Turn the key,' cried Arthur desperately. 'The key, Danny. Turn it! Clever boy. Turn it back!'

There was the scrape of the key in the lock. Arthur held his breath. Then there was a thump as the key fell to the floor on the other side of the door.

Danny began to cry bitterly.

He was lost and wretched, suddenly aware of his loneliness. And out there he could come up against too many perils. He could turn on the gas cooker, do something dangerous with matches . . .

Arthur gave up. He went back to the microphone and said, 'All right. It's a deal.'

He and Miss Mouse went to the window. Miss Mouse. Not Melanie. Not yet.

He opened the window and leaned out. It seemed an age before Mrs. Cobb hobbled painfully across the grass below. Her daughter pressed the key into

Arthur's hand and he dropped it, watching it hit the ground and watching Mrs. Cobb stoop creakingly over it.

She went slowly indoors. There was another terrible gap — an abyss of time — as they waked for her to get into the elevator and come up.

Danny cried steadily.

'It's all right, old boy,' said Arthur through the door. 'Don't cry. It'll be all right in a minute.'

All right? In a minute — in a lifetime — ever again?

Abruptly Miss Mouse's hand closed on his. In a whisper, as though her mother might still hear, she said, 'I'll make it worthwhile for you, Arthur. I promise that. It'll work out. We'll get rid of — of her.' She nodded contemptuously at the corpse stretched out on the bed. 'And then we can be together. And then' — she smiled a dark, possessive, conspiratorial smile — 'we can decide what to do about Mother.'

They heard the front door opening. Footsteps crossed the hall. Danny stopped crying.

'There, now,' Mrs. Cobb wheezed at him. She wheezed again as she stooped to pick up the key for the bedroom door. Then that, too, turned in the lock and she opened the door and beamed at her daughter and Arthur. 'There, now.' This time it was a coo.

All right, thought Arthur. All right! He would play along with them. But once the car was smashed and Lucille smashed inside it, they couldn't touch him. He would deny all accusations. There would be no proof. If he had the strength to stand up to them, the strength to defy them —

'I'm getting old,' said Mrs. Cobb, standing in front of him. 'I've always longed for something to happen. Something. Anything. And now it has. I'm old and I've nothing to lose. If you look after me I'll be happy. If you try to cheat — to back down — I'll tell the truth. No matter what the consequences. Accessory after the fact, all the rest of it — oh, I do read a lot, you know, I understand it all. And I don't care. So don't think you can cheat me. Either way I shall enjoy it. But you two, if you don't play fair — well, it won't be so enjoyable for *you*, will it? For either of you. For both of you.'

There was no apparent menace in her tone. Her old face crinkled into a smile that most people would have found sweet and even lovable. She meant, cheerfully and unequivocally, every word she said.

Miss Mouse's hand remained closed over Arthur's. She was telling him that it was now the two of them against her mother.

And after that? After Mrs. Cobb had somehow or other been dealt with?

Arthur had silenced Lucille once and for all. It was dawning on him that there could be more insistent, more terrifyingly purposeful voices than Lucille's had ever been.

THE END

We do hope that you have enjoyed reading this large print book.

Did you know that all of our titles are available for purchase?

We publish a wide range of high quality large print books including:
Romances, Mysteries, Classics
General Fiction
Non Fiction and Westerns

Special interest titles available in large print are:
The Little Oxford Dictionary
Music Book, Song Book
Hymn Book, Service Book

Also available from us courtesy of Oxford University Press:
Young Readers' Dictionary
(large print edition)
Young Readers' Thesaurus
(large print edition)

For further information or a free brochure, please contact us at:
Ulverscroft Large Print Books Ltd.,
The Green, Bradgate Road, Anstey,
Leicester, LE7 7FU, England.
Tel: (00 44) **0116 236 4325**
Fax: (00 44) **0116 234 0205**